PORTRAIT

in

BLOOD RED

TERÉZIA SZÁSZ

Ordering Information:

Books to Life Marketing Ltd
128 City Road, London, EC1V 2NX, UK

Printed in the United States of America

Portrait in Blood Red

ONE

THAT WAS A boring Tuesday. I woke up at 6 pm as usual, but I lazed for a few minutes—sometimes it's more sometimes it's less. I'm a retired police officer, an old hunting dog and I have plenty of time... Wait a moment! I'm not so old, just forty-five, but a poorly assembled grenade exploded next to me. It was hidden in a dustbin and when I checked the scene I didn't notice right away. Nobody was injured except me. The left side of my face and neck burned, however it's not serious just a dramatic sight, more precisely, it looks like a 3D topographic map. I had a concussion too; I was lying in a hospital bed for two weeks, that's all. The Superintendent decided that I was too shocked and I had psychological damage thus I was not suitable for work. They gently declared this to me, and so I didn't even visit them at the police office.

Normally, after a few months of rehabilitation, you could be repositioned to another police office, or another town—not me. In truth, I'm a workaholic—my colleagues and superiors called me a *busybody*. Nevertheless, I wasn't so popular in City Hall, I mean, among the politicians, since I had some unpleasant cases a few years ago. That grenade affair was an excellent reason for them. 'Sorry... in your state... you have to understand it... it would be better... retired.' Yes, I understand, because I couldn't have done anything else... That was a year ago. I've been in a sort of standby mode ever since. I cannot explain clearly, but I had a special feeling as if I had been waiting for something, perhaps I hoped they would change that whole *retired* thing.

Tuesday. A boring Tuesday. I got out of the bed and went to the bathroom. I ran a few miles, my daily dose—I learnt in a royal military college and I had many bad habits. Afterwards, I took a shower and then came the next item on the agenda. I got dressed up and finally, I put on a dark blue fabric jacket which was like an old-fashioned military coat. I usually had my breakfast in a small Italian coffee shop. They had delicious sandwiches with different types of ham and cheese from Venice—Mr and Mrs Bianchi, the owners, had come from there. I practically lived on that food since I was alone. I divorced after my *accident* because my wife couldn't accept my new face. Don't think she's a heartless person; I suspect she was friendly with that lawyer, whom she later married, before the great explosion.

Queer. That boom changed my life and partly my habits. I had to say goodbye to my office and work—I had been a Chief Inspector with lots of verbal praise without promotion—as follows, my previous life became nothing. Nevertheless, I wanted to avoid idleness; therefore, I planned some new routines for example a slow breakfast and long walks. After my excellent breakfast, I wandered through the streets one after the other. If I stayed home, I would feel empty. On the streets among the people, I didn't think about that, because I observed what happened around me. I liked so much those walks, and I didn't leave them out in the rain or cold.

▪—▪—▪—▪□▪—▪—▪—▪

It was a foggy day. The visibility was limited to a few feet and I hadn't seen anyone for a long time, just a solitary march—it also had its charm.

Suddenly an arm caught my coat.

'Sorry, Mr...' said a voice. After that I could see a man wearing surprisingly colourful clothes.

I didn't say what was more unusual, the movement or that person's appearance.

He had a purple velvet jacket with a great turquoise scarf. His trousers are yellowish green and his shoes shined in burgundy. I didn't have as many colours in my wardrobe as his outfit offered.

'Sorry' repeated he. 'May I introduce myself: my name is Francesco Russo. I'm a painter Mr...'

'Morgan' replied I suspiciously.

'Mr Morgan' smiled at me. 'So Mr Morgan as I mentioned I'm a painter and I have a group, they paint portraits in academic art style, but that isn't important now. However, I think you could be the next model. I have seen you several times traversing this street and I observed that you passed here in the morning. Your face… you know…'

I nodded. If it would have been too embarrassing to say, it wasn't necessary.

'Don't be afraid!' He continued. 'It isn't a nude; you wear whatever clothes you want, I just always ask the same. You sit in an antique armchair motionless; that will be simple. What do you think, Mr Morgan?'

I had free time—that was what I thought.

'You have to know, I'm a retired police officer, Mr Russo, and art is not my forte' explicated I. Honestly the last time—two years ago—I had visited the museum, when the managing director had been murdered with a paper-cutter in his office.

'I don't think it isn't a hindrance' noted Russo. 'You will enjoy it, I think, and you can meet interesting people. What do you say?'

I hesitated a few seconds. About portraits and studios… I remembered well the moral policing education. I'm afraid it would be better if I didn't mention it.

'I have a suggestion' he said, determined not to give up. 'Come to my class this afternoon. Ok?'

'Alright' responded I finally. It didn't matter, did it?

'Marvelous! I will wait for you near to the school building. Do you know where the Hamilton House is?'

'Yes, I do.'

'Well we meet at the Hamilton House at half past two, Mr Morgan. And thank you so much!' he shook my hand.

'At the Hamilton House! Remember!' He waved goodbye and disappeared in the fog.

It crossed my mind not to go to that *rendezvous*; still, I was standing at the Hamilton House when the great, old clock tower started to chime. It was three o'clock punctual. It seemed Mr Russo changed his mind... I decided to give him fifteen minutes. He was an artist thus it was possible he didn't know what the time was.

A few minutes later Russo's colourful figure appeared.

'Mr Morgan, I hope that I would find you here. Sorry for my lateness... Now please follow me' he said, pointing to the left.

We walked across to the other side where a small backstreet was. The school operated in a maroon Victorian building. As I later found out a noble family had had it a long time ago—ladies and lords like in Jane Austin's novel—and after the war it had been a hospital. In the '80s and '90s they closed following that, an arrogant American businessman wanted to buy and build a hotel out of it, finally, City Hall vetoed that project. Nowadays, an art school rented it.

We entered. The last time I had seen so many paintings and sculptures together as in the warehouse of the Department of Stolen Art. From the 18th century till nowadays or something. I suspected the modern ones partly were made by that school's students. On one of them, even the oil paint had not even dried properly yet.

Russo led me into a classroom on the first floor. More precisely, we went up the stairs and he stopped suddenly.

'This is yours' he handed me a book. 'I think you will find it interesting because it also involves a murder... I found some articles about you on the web, and I know already that you worked in Homicide. And I believe you checked my name too, Mr Morgan.'

I didn't feel it would be necessary, because Russo didn't seem abnormal or dangerous. Should I have said I hadn't thought of it? No, it would have been impolite. At last, I made no reply just a half-smile.

'Good' he nodded and pointed to the door. 'Then maybe we should go inside.'

Before I entered the classroom, I quickly read the cover: *Oscar Wilde—The Picture of Dorian Gray*. It was as if I had heard of this book before. I couldn't recall... No! I got it! Many years ago I had seen the movie with my actual girlfriend. I don't remember much... there had been a naive girlish young man who had become a cold-blooded killer. Oh, yes! There had been a painter too in the story... the victim. What can I say? If I examine art from this point of view, it already seems exciting.

By the way, Mr Russo didn't give me much time and he immediately began to speak.

'Ladies and gentlemen, this is Mr Morgan who will be our model in this course. I came up with something special thus it won't be easy for you. Until Mr Morgan takes a seat, you get ready please.'

Then I understood why I received that book. I was *The Reading Man*—I would have given that title. Russo seated me in an armchair and adjusted my shoulders, arms, head and the book in my hand. I couldn't say it was a comfortable pose. While Mr Russo was performing this operation, I looked around carefully.

Five students were standing in front of me: three women and two men. First—yes, first indeed—Lucia Hawkins. Well, she is whom you have to paint, not me. She was beautiful, with dark eyes, dark hair, red lips, nice and elegant. I liked watching her. She smiled at me, and I smiled back. To her right there was a pale timid blondie, I didn't know her name. To Lucia Hawkins' left a grey-haired cheerful guy was wearing a pink checkered sweater with his younger friend—two gay guys: Mr Brown and Mr Felton. They were enthusiastic and at the same time a little bit disappointed when they found out I wouldn't undress. The fifth student was a passionate woman, Mrs Alford. It seemed to me she was the oldest pupil of Mr Russo, I mean she had completed several courses; besides, she wanted to take my clothes off—I had a feeling that it was not allowed from an artistic method. Mrs Alford's costume bloomed many giant peach-coloured roses—like a costume really from a cheap play. Otherwise, Mrs Alford was the only one who helped Russo. She touched me and caressed me; as if I were a vegetable in the market.

Finally, Mr Russo found my pose suitable and the students started to draw the sketch thus I began to read. Classical music played softly from a machine, and sometimes whispers were heard, however, I progressed quite slowly with the book. My thoughts always wandered; mainly towards Lucia Hawkins. I couldn't see her, namely, I had to stare at the pages, but I smelt her perfume and so it was not easy to concentrate on the text. I didn't know how much time had passed, but I was just at the end of chapter one when Mr Russo spoke unexpectedly:

'Ladies and gentlemen, break time.'

I moved my stiff arms and followed the students to the tea table. There I introduce myself with many *nice to meet yous*. Mrs Alford told me that the school serviced the tea and Mr Brown the biscuit—he was an excellent cake maker. He made lemon, almond and chocolate ones—but I guessed Mr Felton had helped him. So, I tasted a lemon one with my tea and a few minutes later I found myself in the middle of a bizarre conversation.

'I cannot agree with you, Miss Trenton' Mr Brown said, the cake maker in a pink checkered sweater. 'Mr Morgan looks like *Hamlet* rather. His speechlessness hides a serious drama, I think.'

Marie Trenton was the timid blondie.

'No, Mr Brown, you're wrong' replied Miss Trenton with a thin voice. 'Mr Morgan has a piercing gaze, he hides passion, some dark secret. I think *Macbeth*, not *Hamlet*.'

'Yes! Full of passion!' cried Mrs Alford emotionally and she winked at me. 'I'm sure Mr Morgan is a complex personality full of… passion' she repeated full of… heat.

And as she said that *passion*—I bet—she had dozen of romance novels going through her mind.

After then, I was everything; the complete works of Shakespeare except *Richard the Third*. I didn't want to interfere, so I just sipped my tea quietly.

'Maybe we should ask Mr Morgan himself.' Of course, Lucia Hawkins suggested it. 'Well, Mr Morgan, which Shakespeare's character are you?' She looked straight at me with her deep brown eyes.

'I must disappoint you, but I have never thought of this before' I replied politely. The answer *I have no idea* couldn't be convenient.

'I see' Russo stepped next to me—he had a special flair for solving awkward situations. 'Mr Morgan prefers the Robert Louis Stevenson's characters, I think. Not *Long John Silver*, I suspect, *Allan Breck Stewart*.'

I cannot deny that Stevenson is closer to my heart than Shakespeare. At the same time, I knew well if I started to dispute it would have never ended and that was the only solution being permissive.

'It's correct, Mr Russo. I liked *Kidnapped*, it is a very thrilling story' I nodded.

Lucia Hawkins looked at me so suspiciously and noticed:

'Your response is enigmatic, Mr Morgan.'

Yes, I know. That was what I wanted.

TWO

SINCE THEN EVERY Tuesday and Friday I have gone to the art school on the first floor. I enjoyed these classes: reading my book and the break time with tea and cake, although, I was an observer in the company so I could make a few judgements.

1. The relationship between Brown and Felton wasn't equal. Brown's attachment was stronger and he was older, for Felton just comfortable. Brown acted like a father and lover in all in one until Felton just accepted that—he was a spoiled child. Felton would likely finish that connection if he received a *better offer.* And just one more thing: while Mr Brown was an excellent but amateur art historian and artist, Mr Felton was less interested in the arts.

2. Miss Trenton avoided the company of men. Russo is an exception to this, as he was an artist; and Brown too—it didn't need an explanation. Dubious thing, she feared Felton, she pulled away

from him during the break time at the tea table. She was afraid of me—of course—because of my face and my identity. I had seen similar behaviour before. I think Miss Trenton had a violent man in her life, her father or a boyfriend. I saw the fear in her eyes when she looked at me.

3.   Mrs Alford. Sophia. According to her admission, she has had four husbands: three divorces and one funeral. Those men didn't know what they were doing or very much so. She is said to be rich. Unlike Miss Trenton, Mrs Alford loved the men's company. She flirted equally with Russo, Brown and Felton too—and me. She often noted that she was single and smiled at me seductively.

4.   Russo, the Master. He was a great artist with an empty pocket. He had exhibitions, yes, but he hadn't sold too many pictures. That could also be an explanation for why he often aids other people and why he's a selfless person. Russo had a habit of giving away his works. I received one, a copy of Lady Worsley's portrait. Russo painted just the upper part of the original, the head and the chest. He said I certainly understood that woman—I searched a little bit, and I think so. I put that painting on the living room wall.

5.   Lucia Hawkins. I didn't know much about her—I didn't even try very hard to find out. She completely charmed me, and I wanted to preserve the illusion. If I found out later she is the black

widow—no problem. Apropos, she had a husband, Michael, a bookkeeper. It sounded dull, but they said he was a happy fellow and loved Lucia so much. I can understand it… and there went my *great expectations*.

Sometimes, others joined that course, often three young women. They were fun and noisy. Russo told me that they came from the University of Fine Arts. They laughed a lot and painted little. There was also an old meticulous man, Mr Stevenson. He was never satisfied with his work and used a lot of turpentine; but it was mostly women of different ages, none of whom were particularly remarkable.

During the tea time, I observed the sketches and painting very carefully—of course. I'm not an art historian, my comment is *absolutely* private. Mr Brown painted me in a realistic style—perhaps I seemed too gloomy; while Mrs Alford in romantic idealism—I've never been so handsome. Miss Trenton used weak brush strokes and pastel colours; Lucia Hawkins worked precisely but without emotion; and Felton's performance was like a child's drawing. About Mr Stevenson, well, when he finally finished a part, he began with a turpentine rag. And the three girls… I think that's how I would look after drinking three bottles of gin; Mr Russo said that was the cubism.

The smell of oil paint spread in the classroom. I obediently posed as Mr Russo had set me. I read chapter seven, the dialogue between Dorian Gray and Basil Hallward—that was the painter. Hallward wanted to take the picture to an exhibit, but Dorian Gray wanted to hide it, and I wanted to turn the page when a curious incident happened, as we had an unexpected visitor: a tall, skinny man with long grey hair and a bushy beard. He was drunk and completely naked. He staggered into the middle of the classroom and then pulled Mr Russo's jacket.

'How dare you? You… you housepainter… you… nothing… This body…' he hit his chest and straightened. 'This body was exhibited in the Tate Gallery. And you? You chose that…' At that moment, he pointed to me 'that ordinary creature. You can't do that! You will regret… Understand? You-will-reg-ret!'

'You have drunk so much, Jake' Russo replied in a calm voice. 'Go home and sleep.'

'No!' cried the naked Jake and looked around. He noticed Miss Trenton turned her head away. 'What's wrong, honey? Do you want a special tutorial course with me?' he grinned with a drunken smile.

'Enough, Jake! Go home, drink a strong coffee, but first get dressed.'

Russo drove the naked man from our classroom and finally, he closed the door.

'Sorry about this. Jake is a good boy when he is sober' Russo excused himself. 'But nowadays he has been drinking too much…'

'Drinking? More like bathing in alcohol. He smells like a beer barrel' Mrs Alford remarked dryly. 'Satyr!'

'I think we should take a break now' said Mr Russo.

I started to exercise my numbed arms.

'Who was that?' I asked after I poured myself a cup of tea.

'Jake Swanson, a famous nude model. He was so popular a few years ago' explained Mr Brown.

'Infamous, not famous' noted Mrs Alford. 'He keeps trying to seduce me... all the time—You can imagine!'

I didn't want to imagine.

THREE

'WHERE ARE MR Brown and Mr Felton?' Mrs Alford asked turning her head curiously like a giant cat. She was a few minutes late so she could reasonably assume that everyone else had already arrived.

'Mr Brown called me ten minutes ago. He's ill, he cannot come today' replied Russo.

'And Mr Felton?' Mrs Alford continued to question.

'He is caring for Mr Brown, I think.'

'Queer thing! Mr Brown has not been missed a session, not even once. Do you remember? Last year he had that hard cold, he still came.' Lucia Hawkins' words were somewhat troubling.

'We can visit them after classes' spoke timidly Miss Trenton.

'Excellent idea!' approved Russo and all of us agreed.

We had shorter classes and just a five-minute break. Mr Russo didn't want the two missing students to suffer a disadvantage. After then, we set off, and from a nearby restaurant Mrs Alford got a very delicious soup as medicine.

Mr Brown's flat was a few minutes' walk from the school building. We went up the second floor and Mr Russo rang the bell. We waited, but nothing. Russo rang again.

'Perhaps Mr Felton went to the pharmacy or shopping and Mr Brown is sleeping' he explained and tried once more... nothing. 'If Mr Brown is sleeping, don't disturb him. Give the soup to the neighbour.'

We made a pilgrimage to the next door. A grey-haired sorceress' face appeared—I mean that old lady looked like a witch from a Grimm tale. She had a squawking voice.

'What do you want? I don't buy anything.'

'Terrible sorry, Mme' started Russo. 'We're friends of Mr Brown and...'

'Its comings and goings all day. In the morning that young man moved away. Those men made the whole staircase dirty. And now you. It's scandalous! I will fill a complaint!' she cawed and slammed the door.

That young man moved away—that was Felton. Gosh! I had a bad feeling. There was no time to explain. Mr Brown's door—and presumably the locks too—was an old type. I had dealt with something similar, and I had a sure way to get into the flat: the raw violence. I broke it down with a few powerful kicks.

Brown was not in the bedroom or the bathroom. I found him in the kitchen sitting at the table. He stared straight ahead. On the table were pills and a glass of water.

He looked at me very slowly.

'I cannot do this' he sighed painfully.

I swept the pills into my palm and hurried to the bathroom to flush down the toilet. When I got back, he was sitting there and repeated:

'I cannot do this… I cannot…'

'What's happened?' asked Russo in a gently voice like a doctor to the patient.

'I think it would be better that I made some tea' Mrs Alford proposed and grabbed the teapot at once. 'Oh, Mr Brown, you made muffins! Great!'

And really. And really, the muffins were waiting—packed and ready to go. I had seen several times the suicides had done their housework carefully—washing, ironing, or making dinner—before… That was what immediately came to my mind.

Mr Russo and Mrs Alford offered consolation for the broken heart. Miss Trenton—it was she who fully felt Mr Brown's suffering—cried quietly. Lucia Hawkins tried to comfort her.

Mr Brown told to us, after breakfast—excellent timing—Felton announced to leave Brown… just like that. So, I think he had the *better offer* indeed.

'What will I do? I won't find anybody who loves me… I'm nothing without him…'

'That's not true! You are a very valuable man, Mr Brown' stated Russo.

'But is it possible to live without love?' asked Brown bitterly.

'No, it isn't possible' Mrs Alford replied and sighed heavily as if she was the one who had been left.

I think life without love moves perfectly well, but I didn't want to spoil that sentimental mood. I began to feel as if I had fallen into a very dramatic BBC series.

'You didn't match each other, Mr Brown' I noted in a low voice hoping he could hear that.

'What do you mean, Mr Morgan?' Brown turned to me.

'Sorry, I didn't want...' I started to apologize. I didn't want to speak about my private statements.

'No, please. I'm interested in your opinion.' It seemed that Mr Brown's curiosity was genuine.

I thought I couldn't have made it any worse.

'As I saw it, you gave it your all, Felton just wasn't it. He's what you would call a *bel ami*... Sorry... My ex-wife always told me how insensitive I am. Sorry' I explained quickly because I was a little embarrassed; everyone was looking at me.

Mr Brown spoke a few seconds later.

'Thank you, Mr Morgan, for your frankness... and help too.'

'As a matter of fact, I owe you a front door, Mr Brown' I grimaced. 'I broke it.'

'You broke down my door?' Brown asked, amazed. Then he started to laugh. 'That was a burglar-proof door, and you broke it.'

I didn't understand what was so funny; everyone else was laughing. Sometimes people can react strangely to strong emotional influence.

FOUR

MR RUSSO ORGANIZED a special class in the nearby gallery—probably he wanted to cheer up Mr Brown. Russo invited me, saying *I am a classmate too*—it was like a school trip. I didn't argue; maybe I could learn something—who knows?

On Monday we gathered in the front of the school building, and we took a longer walk to the gallery. Russo led us to the back entrance. As it turned out we were not visiting the current exhibitions, but the restorer's workshop and the warehouse. We had to wear protective clothing—as in a crime scene, so, I liked it. Russo introduced a strict woman, Mrs Robinson, who was the chief of the team. Mrs Robinson showed us every step of restoration, she spoke so much while she watched us to see if we caused any trouble or not.

After then, Mrs Robinson took us to the warehouse where they stored the unexhibited part of the collection. Everybody was delighted... maybe not me so much, but everyone else. Mrs Robinson noticed that she kept asking questions, testing me, and seemed very pleased when I didn't know the answer—just line in physics class.

On the next Tuesday, I started to read chapter twelve and I progressed very slowly because I listened to the conversation.

'I have never touched a Botticelli before! Amazing!' Mr Brown enthused very much. 'What colours! Fantastic!'

'Beautiful.' Miss Trenton had that low-key comment.

Afterwards, Mr Russo gave us a lecture on the oil paint-making technique of the Renaissance masters. It not had been easy for them; however, they had ordered that making to their *famulus* who often had painted instead of his master. It was a dangerous profession because they had used mercury.

At the end of the class, a few pages and the last chapter remained from *Dorian Gray*.

'You will finish it on Friday however our paintings are just beginning to form' noted Russo. 'Next time I have to give a new book and I already know which one' added he suspiciously.

I didn't understand exactly why I had to read *Dorian Gray* or anything else, but I obeyed because he was the teacher and I... something like a student.

After class, Mr Brown asked me to stay; he wanted to speak with me. We walked to the end of the corridor.

'Mr Morgan…' started he.

'Yes. I know… the door' nodded I. 'How much…?'

Mr Brown smiled.

'I was warned you don't like being thanked, but I'll do it, Mr Morgan. Sorry. I thought a lot about what you said. It was bitter medicine for me; I still think you're right. Thank you again, Mr Morgan. You're a good man' he shook my hand.

I would rather pay for the door. I don't like *thank yous*.

FIVE

I WAS SO curious about what kind of reading Mr Russo had chosen so I arrived earlier. When I entered the classroom, I noticed Lucia Hawkins, Miss Trenton, Mrs Alford, and Mr Brown. Mr Russo wasn't there, perhaps he was late. They all seemed to be so sad. Mr Brown spoke first.

'Did you hear about it?'

'No. What?'

'Mr Russo died on Wednesday' answered Brown mournfully. 'I baked a cheesecake, for him. This is… was his favourite. Oh, my God!'

'What happened? I don't understand.' I was confused. 'Heart attack or stroke? He looked very healthy and cheerful.' I turned to Lucia Hawkins perhaps she could reply to my questions.

'They said it was suicide' explained Mrs Alford in a dramatic tone. 'He cut his veins sitting in a tub like ancient Romans. It's terrible!'

'Nonsense, I cannot believe' answered I.

'That's right! I said that same thing a few minutes ago' noted Brown. 'Mr Russo could not commit suicide.'

'Who told that? I mean those details about Mr Russo's death' demanded I; as if an alarm clock started to ring in my head.

'That selfish arrogant woman' responded Brown.

'Who?'

'His widow, Mrs Russo. They had never divorced' commented Mrs Alford. 'She called the school director this morning.'

His widow? Russo never mentioned that he had a wife. I wondered, but it was true I knew him only superficially.

'That woman left him a year and a half ago and moved to France with a businessman—he has an electronics company if I remember well. I never understood why they got married, Russo and that woman, you know. They had nothing in common. Mr Russo was a sensitive artist… that woman… she's cold and emotionless as a machine.' Brown didn't like Mrs Russo.

So there was a widow. As far as I could tell, Russo wasn't very wealthy but I didn't like that *cut-veins* thing. I didn't fit the picture.

'I think it would be better to look into it' I suggested after some thought.

Suddenly there was an awkward silence.

'I feel sorry for Mr Russo… I agreed with Michael' started Lucia Hawkins. 'Whatever happened we cannot change it and I signed up for Miss Primrose's class.'

Yes, Michael, the excellent bookkeeper and perfect husband. He always knows everything. I admit I was disappointed in Lucia Hawkins then. I was hoping she was adventurous; however, this was obviously out of the question. She put on her coat and handbag.

'Bye!' she waved at us and left.

'I think Lucia's right' said a timid voice, Miss Trenton. 'I'm going. See you later!' She clutched her belongings like a terrified child and hurried after Lucia Hawkins.

And then there were... three of us.

'So...' I would have begun, but Mrs Alford was faster.

'I knew you wouldn't leave it at all. You'll investigate, won't you, Mr Morgan? You're a real detective. I mean it's in your blood.'

I couldn't deny it.

'I must see the body and the scene... and, Mr Brown, I'm afraid your cake will play an important role.' I already had the whole plan in my head. It was automatic, and the button had been pressed.

'You mean I have to see the body?' Brown turned pale.

'No, Mr Brown.'

'Thanks God!'

∎—∎—∎—∎▢∎—∎—∎—∎

Mrs Alford offered her car, a cherry red SAAB—I think she didn't want to miss anything—thus we made a little trip to the morgue. Doctor Robertson owed me half a dozen favours. Robertson was Professor Grant's assistant; he worked at that spooky place and had an extraordinary sweet tooth. Me, and Mr Brown's magnificent cheesecake sneaked off to his office. If I calculated well the Professor already gone, but Robertson should still be in there. It was about 4 pm and you have to know the old mummy—as Robertson named the Professor—always went to his golf club on Friday afternoon.

I knocked at the door. A few seconds later Robertson's face appeared. He seemed irritated and when he glanced at me, he smiled for a moment.

'I have said several times, do not disturb if there is a consultation' he spoke loudly. 'In an hour in the pub' he added softly. 'What's this?'

'Cheesecake with lemon.'

'Wait a moment' he closed the door. 'What do you want?'

'Russo's case.'

'Right. Give me the cake and wait in the pub.'

I nodded.

'What's up?' asked Mrs Alford excitedly when I returned.

'We'll meet later. In the meantime, how about I invite you to lunch?' I didn't know why, I became hungry as a wolf.

'You're very kind, Mr Morgan. Thank you' answered Mrs Alford gently.

'It will be nice' noted Brown. 'Has he tasted my cake yet?'

Tasted? I guessed Robertson had already eaten it all.

■—■—■—■□■—■—■—■

I managed to talk them into choosing the steak pie which was the most delicious and—for that reason—the most popular food in that pub. I drank tonic water, Brown sipped his first Guinness while Mrs Alford was at the end of her second glass—and already ordered the third one.

'When I'm nervous, I'm thirsty' explicated she.

A few minutes later they brought the pies.

'Bon appetite' I said and cut into the hot pastry with my knife.

'*Bon appétit!* said Mr. Brown with French accent. 'This smell is mouth-watering.'

'Bon appetite, gentlemen. Where is my next Guinness?'

By the time Robertson sat down next to me, I had already finished my food. I always eat so fast—this is one of my bad habits. I let him court Mrs Alford and praise Brown's masterpiece. After then, Robertson gave me Russo's autopsy report.

'I'll wait for it, I'll eat something until then' whispered he. 'You have twenty minutes.'

That time was enough. First, I looked at the pictures. Robertson attached a few which had been taken at the crime scene. Russo sat in his tub, blood was in the water, on the tiles. As far as I could see it was a well-directed stage—not lifelike, however, everything was right: the cuts, the position of the body, the hot water and the locked doors. Next to the tub, there was a small table with a tray, and on it were an empty bottle of Chianti and a glass full of Russo's fingerprints and red wine.

'He had a good taste' said Robertson.

'Are you thinking of the wine type?'

'No. I think of his wife. *Bellissima.*'

'Beauty is not everything' interrupted Mr Brown. 'Be careful, young man, that woman is a sneak.'

Afterwards, they argued about the question of *Beauty and the Beast*, while I read the autopsy report. That was a suicide unquestionably—wrote the Professor—and the facts also supported this: the direction of the cuts, the traces of blood and so on, but I did not take it. Maybe there was no contradiction in that autopsy report, but between my knowledge and Russo's death, there was.

SIX

WE AGREED THAT the next morning Mrs Alford, Mr Brown and I would meet near the Russo's house. He lived in the suburb, a charming building which had been built in '70s. It had a typical brick wall with ivy and other sprawling vegetation. I arrived first, so I took a good look around. There no were *CRIME SCENE DO NOT CROSS* tape or similar. It was queer. Nay! There was a billboard next to the entrance:

Taylor Real State Office—Trust me! I'll find your perfect home. Call me now...

So, I trusted him and I called the phone number immediately. By the time Mrs Alford's SAAB stopped in front of the house, I already had an appointment with Mr Taylor.

'He'll be here in twenty minutes' I said after I explained the new situation. 'This was a crime scene three days ago. They should have judicial permission; otherwise, they wouldn't have been able to do this so quickly. Things are moving too fast.'

'That heartless woman!' noted Mr Brown. He wore a burgundy suit, pink shirt with an unspecified colour tie and shoes. It seemed he couldn't leave his favourite tone.

'How did she get that permission?' Mrs Alford asked, adjusting her provocative wide-brimmed red hat; however, she dressed in black that morning. I think she wanted to add a little liveliness to that extreme piece in her appearance.

'I think she had much money and a good relationship, I think' I replied while noticing a woman's face in the upstairs window of the neighbouring house. That blond-haired young woman watched us. Maybe we had finished our investigation of Russo's rooms, and we should visit her.

Taylor was punctual and drove an Aston Martin—perhaps his business could be going well, or he was just a great *James Bond* fan, who knows?

'I'm not surprised your call, Mr Morgan' he said, and started to open the front door. 'I've just been advertising for one day, but I have already had six inquiries. You're a very lucky man, Mr Morgan. They finished the cleaning yesterday evening and you're the first one who can see this wonderful, charming place.'

Perfect. *You had to let Taylor talk because he is a long-winded person.* Interpreting what I heard: Mrs Russo had judicial permission, and ordered the cleaning and buying yesterday, on Friday, two days after her *beloved* husband's death. Mrs Russo was in a hurry for some reason. Nevertheless, I already knew Mrs and Mr Russo hadn't any child or other relatives. It seemed Mrs Russo was the only heiress; she could not count on great wealth. Russo rented that house, no bonds, no life insurance; just old furniture, oil paintings and so on.

'This way' entered Taylor, our special guide. 'This is the dining room...'

That was the second oddity: everything was clear and new—I mean the furniture, the curtains, carpets, everything. I didn't expect such a crime scene and I was sure I would not find any trace there. Moreover, there was not a painting in sight. There was no sign that a painter had ever lived in that house.

Taylor just talked and talked, but his speech didn't make much sense.

'May I see the bathroom? You know, I think the bathroom is the most important place in my home. I like reading in the tub' I interrupted, because I hoped to find something... maybe.

'Of course, Mr Morgan. Please follow me. This way' nodded Taylor.

Mrs Alford and Mr Brown stayed in the living room. I thought they might not want to see the place where Mr Russo had died. I was motivated by curiosity; they were motivated by grief and disgust.

The bathroom was the most sterile scene which I'd ever seen before; the tiles shone, new selves, towels, fresh fruit-scented soap as in a first classed hotel's royal suite.

'This is an old-style one, but the water pipes were replaced a few years ago. Very comfortable, Mr. Morgan. What do you think?'

What did I think? If someone suspected Russo's death, he could not prove his truth. I wouldn't be surprised if they already had cremated the body—that was what I thought.

'I must see the kitchen' I answered finally.

'And now, Mr Morgan?' questioned Taylor a few minutes later. He was a leech and he wanted to sell that haunted house.

'The kitchen is too small and dark' snapped Mr Brown—fortunately, because I couldn't tell anything.

'And the bedroom also' added Mrs Alford.

I couldn't imagine what Taylor thought of us—a woman in black with a red hat, a man in burgundy and pink, and another one with a burnt face, strange *menagerie*—but he realized I wasn't his ideal customer.

'In an hour, a nice couple will come to buy it. So if you aren't interested...'

'Yes... I mean, no. We won't bother you anymore, Mr Taylor. And thank you for your time' I said, and we shook hands.

The Aston Martin slowly disappeared. I noticed the young woman watching us again. I turned toward her window and I looked straight at her. She unexpectedly smiled at me and waved.

'I think that young woman wants to talk to us' I pointed to the neighbouring house.

'Oh, yes! Mrs Simpson. I know her; she's a kind young woman. Her husband is a car mechanic, a really handyman, he regularly fixes my SAAB. They had five children, five little devils, and a whole nursery. They are always cheerful yet… well, they are a lovely family. Mr Russo often talked about them' said Mrs Alford and started towards the Simpson's house.

A few minutes later we were in a large living room which was rather a playground full of children's toys and fairy tale books. I sat in a comfortable armchair in the company of a giant teddy bear with a cup of tea and chocolate biscuits. Mrs Alford and Brown got a place on a floral-patterned sofa.

Mr Simpson and the older four children had gone shopping, and Mrs Simpson stayed at home with the fifth one, who had a toothache. The fifth one was quiet then, because he was scared of the strangers.

'I recognised you immediately, Mrs Alford, because of your beautiful hat.' Mrs Simpson had a pleasant voice. 'You always look so elegant!… If I guess correctly you come for the death of Mr. Russo.'

'Yes, darling. You're right… Terrible thing' answered Mrs Alford.

'Yes, it is. Terrible and very suspicious' nodded Mrs Simpson while she nourished the youngest Simpson who uncertainly eyed us. There was some yellowish liquid in the baby bottle. 'We heard what happened on Thursday morning from the constable posted in front of the house' continued she. 'We couldn't believe… The charwoman found him. Poor Mr Russo!… After then, the police cars came and they brought the body away in a black sack. I was shocked… Johnny and I don't understand… Suicide? Impossible!'

Johnny Simpson was the husband, but there was another Johnny in that family; the youngest Simpson who was feeding very peacefully at that moment. He probably realized we were not a threat to his baby bottle.

'After that…' told Mrs Simpson 'yesterday those men came by with great vans. They gave away the most of furniture, Mr Russo's paintings. I mean his collection and his ones…'

I am sorry; I didn't mention before that Russo had a small and modest collection of XVIII-century English painters. Modest, yes, as those masters were not very well known—neither is J. M. W. Turner. If I remember well there were about seven or ten woman portraits… a few hundred pounds.

'They packed them all morning. The old ones went away and the new ones came in' commented Mrs Simpson. 'Finally, they left some furniture, books, oil paint, easel and other equipment on the street. I called Johnny by phone and we took them into the garage. We didn't want to throw them away… Mr Russo was a kind, funny man, you know. He often had dinner with us and made many drawings and watercolours about the children… Please, come with me' she stood up and led us upstairs. The corridor wall and the children's rooms were lined with Russo's works. Colourful and joyful pictures. 'I have to admit, we placed his favourite armchair in our bedroom and his reading lamp in children's one. If his wife claims them…'

I don't think that would happen.

'You did well' declared Mrs Alford. 'I'm sure Mr Russo would want that.'

'Do you think?'

'Yes, darling.'

'Yes, of course' added Mr Brown and I nodded in confirmation.

Then Mrs Simpson showed the garage.

'We put his stuff in boxes. Here the books are, there are the oil paint's tubes, brushes and other things... I didn't know what we do with them... maybe somebody uses...'

'I think the students would be happy' suggested Mrs Alford. 'I'll take them after the funeral... and we'll make a memorial corner in our classroom.'

'Wonderful idea!' enthused Mr Brown.

'There are his clothes' pointed Mrs Simpson a large paper box. 'I remember he always wore a jacket when he painted.'

'The ocher one?' asked Mrs Alford.

'Yes, the ocher... You know, I was relieved to be able to talk to you... And you, Mr Morgan, I think, that is yours.' Mrs Simpson opened a smaller box and took out a book from it. 'It was on top of the pile.'

That was a volume with a piece of paper on which my name was written: *Sean Morgan*.

'What is it?' asked Mrs Alford.

'*James Wilson: The Dark Clue*... a novel about paintings' replied I after reading the back cover's text.

Suddenly the realization hit me like a bolt of lightning: that was the only evidence of Russo's murder. He wanted to give me that book on Friday. Why did he struggle with its selection and put a paper in it, if he planned his death on Wednesday? After then, I remembered what I thought in Mr Brown's flat that sad evening about that mental state.

'You're right?' whispered Brown. 'You're so pale.'

'Yes... I'm right... Just this book...'

I must have looked pretty weird because Mrs Simpson hugged me and kissed my face. She hugged me as far as the young Johnny Simpson allowed.

'It's too hard, I know...' she said gently.

She didn't even know how right she was. An investigation without traces and witnesses is a very hard thing... really. Suddenly I received some yellowish material on my coat. The youngest Simpson resented me.

'Sorry... I'll clean it quickly' Mrs Simpson looked at me in alarm.

'Don't bother. I like this colour' I tried to make a joke out of it.

Mrs Simpson was relentless about spots. She pulled me into the bathroom and started to remove them with a sponge while Mrs Alford undertook feeding the youngest Simpson.

'Did the police question that man?' noted Mrs Simpson and she washed the sponge again.

'Which man?' I got my head up.

'The person who visited Mr Russo late at night before his death.'

'What did he look like?'

'Like a homeless' answered she. 'A tall skinny man with long grey hair. He seemed very upset and angry, rang several times and shouted. I think he was drunk, he was tilting left and right.

No doubt—that was Jake Swanson probably dressed up this time.

'What did he shout?'

'I could not hear clearly...*You cannot do this, you owe me* or something similar... I said that to the police officer and he wrote in his notebook. It would be good to know if they could talk to him or not... Maybe it is important, isn't it?'

Maybe.

∎—∎—∎—∎□∎—∎—∎—∎

We obtained much information—not exactly as I planned. The next step was meeting Swanson, however, I could not imagine where and when. Mr Brown invited us to lunch. Mrs Alford already had a rendezvous thus said goodbye and got into her SAAB. Before that, she made us promise, we would do nothing without her. I promised, but I couldn't be sure to keep it.

Mr Brown and I walked to the next bus stop.

'What are you thinking about, Mr Morgan?'

'I should find Swanson.'

'It's very simple' stopped Brown suddenly. 'I don't know where he is in the daytime, in turn, I know where he would be in the evenings. Mr Russo once told me what Swanson's favourite pub is. Swanson and the owner are old fellows. Cheap prices with unpleasant clients. It is better to avoid such a place.'

'In this case, I will go alone.'

'I cannot allow it, Mr Morgan. I will go with you' Mr Brown stated firmly. 'I think we should just tell Mrs Alford this tomorrow morning' added he.

On my part, I was more worried about Brown than Mrs Alford.

After our quick travel, we entered a familiar French restaurant. Mr Brown suggested the snails in garlic butter, but I chose some food with potatoes that the waiter named *gratin*. Sorry, my taste is conventional. In return, I let Mr Brown choose among the wine types and desserts.

While we waited for our course, I checked out the location of Swanson's headquarters. Brown was right; it was not the best neighbourhood and was prominent in police statistics.

That *gratin* and the other dishes were delicious, and Mr Brown tried to be a witty conversationalist. It wasn't his fault that I did an interrogation. It was instinctive: I just took out my pen and notebook and started asking many questions. Fortunately, he didn't take it to heart, and even he joked about it.

'Duty is your *hors d'oeuvre, n'est-ce pas, Monsieur* Morgan?' What can I say? Yes.

■—■—■—■□■—■—■—■

Our evening program began at 8 pm thus I had plenty of free time to browse the web. I was not interested in current politics or stock exchange rates; I was haunted by something about Mr Russo's death. Finally, I found a wordy article on a local newspaper's site. There were plenty of irrelevant facts and a few useful ones. According to that article's writer, the investigation was led by a certain Superintendent Charles Laverton. I knew him well, but I couldn't say we were *buddies*. I already understood why Robertson was so careful regarding Russo's autopsy report. Laverton didn't say too much in that article and—I thought—he already decided to close that case. Bad news. I hoped Swanson knew something.

■—■—■—■□■—■—■—■

We entered the pub at 8:15 pm. Many students were searching for something dangerous, and some others wanted to help them. At first glance, I recognized about twenty people from police records. Three of them recognized me, too, and disappeared immediately.

Swanson wasn't there, so we had to wait. I ordered two beers and we sat down at the table near the hallway leading to the toilets, which was also the emergency exit. In my experience, VIP guests prefer to leave there.

'It's terrible! This beer I mean' noted Brown quietly.

I nodded. That beer was horrible indeed and I hopped the counter boy hadn't pissed in it.

Half an hour and four sips of beer later I spotted Swanson's grey hair and bushy beard. I turned my face away in a hurry. He walked over to the counter and ordered something then looked around. A few minutes later Swanson went to a table with a beer mug in his hand. He sat down and started to talk to someone.

'Stay here please' I turned toward Brown and stood up very slowly.

I guessed Swanson wouldn't want to cooperate, but I didn't expect him to throw his mug at me, push me up and run to the toilets—the emergency exit, yes. Although Swanson's nude was more famous in Europe, it was who ran several miles every morning. I caught him within 100 yards. I twisted his arm back and pushed him against the wall—routine.

'If the Russian send you, I cannot pay yet' he squeezed out.

I made no reply.

'If you're a cop, I know my rights' continued Swanson.

I chose the latter option and twisted his arm once more. It was a remarkably useful method when conducting an illegal interrogation.

'I have a few questions about your visit to Francesco Russo.'

'What? Are you mad? I don't know why he killed himself. When I left him, he was alive, I swear!' He barked like a dog. 'I swear!'

I twisted again.

'Right! Right, pal! I stole a silver cigarette case, that's all. He was alive, I swear. We talked, I asked for money, he gave me £50 and I went to the pub. That's all, I swear!'

'And you stole his stuff.'

'I wanted to give back... I want...'

'Was he alone?'

'Yes, I couldn't see anybody… he was working on that stupid painting.'

'Which one?'

'A boring landscape, I don't know…'

I let go of his arm.

'Get out.'

Swanson didn't hesitate too much and ran as he could.

Mr Brown stood a few yards away and looked at me amazed. Until that moment he must have thought I was a polite policeman. He was wrong.

SEVEN

MRS ALFORD WAS slightly offended because she was left out of the *Saturday Fever*; moreover, her rendezvous went terribly. On Sunday we had a conference call and discussed our investigation. We stated only having circumstantial evidence like the book, Swanson's testimony and our conviction. Mrs Alford suggested going to the police and talking with Superintendent Laverton—yes, she had read that article too. I thought it better not to mention that I knew the Superintendent, otherwise, I hadn't any better idea, and I hoped maybe Laverton listened to me.

On Monday morning, I put on my dark grey suit with a characterless tie and a steel-grey shirt. I thought that was pretty official. With Russo's second book, I went to the police station. In the front of the building, I met Mr Brown, who looked like a graduation student: black suit and white shirt. I suspected he knew that Laverton-type well. On the other hand, Mrs Alford wore a blue floral dress with an orange coat. She was striking.

I figured Laverton should be in his office around 10 pm.

The duty officer saluted, gave us access cards, and commanded a young constable to lead us to Laverton's office. On the way, I met Constable Heather O'Neil in the corridor. Before my grenade accident, I had suggested she pass the Sergeants' Exam—as I saw her rank, Laverton could have vetoed it. Heather was a smart and lively girl with red curly hair and many freckles.

'Constable O'Neil' said I.

'Mr Morgan' she answered measuredly not looking at me. Perhaps she hurried maybe.

I didn't think much of it, I was nervous; nevertheless, I tried to stay calm… I'm afraid I forgot to say, it had been Laverton who ordered me to that fatal dustbin where I had met that grenade. No one should have been there, but he had to send me to check the scene and then *the incident* had happened. What can I say? We hadn't even liked each other before.

Laverton didn't welcome us right away—of course. We had to sand in the corridor for at least half an hour. Finally, he invited only me.

'I was anxiously waiting for you to come, Morgan' he grinned as I entered. 'Any big deal? Let me guess! You found the Lindbergh baby's grandson who lives somewhere in Scotland and plays bagpipe.'

He hadn't changed anything; he was the same blockhead as twelve months ago.

'Sir, I have some information about the Russo case' started I.

'The Russo case? You're late. I closed it five minutes ago.'

'With respect, Sir, listen to me...'

'No! You listen to me, Mr Morgan. You're not a police officer anymore. Do you understand it? But maybe... I'm in a good mood...'

He loved those kinds of games and adored his voice, finally, he allowed me to speak. I told him about the art school, Mr Russo's character—how I saw him—, the second book with that piece of paper, the not-quite-legal testimony of Swanson, our conviction and murder theory, and at last, my opinion about the fast cleaning in Russo house.

'If you examine those facts you will admit, Sir, Russo could not have committed suicide' I summarized my arguments.

"I expected some similar lunacy' replied Laverton who had been watching with interest. 'I was sure you wouldn't *rest in peace*. That poor guy... Who did kill him and why?... The doors and windows were closed; he was alone in the house. Alone—I repeat, Mr Morgan. Anyway, artists are passionate and unpredictable. As above, so too below. He was below... that's all.'

I didn't suggest; he offered me a cup of tea, but it seemed that Laverton didn't want anything else—just to rival me, not to catch a murderer.

'Who did kill him?—you asked me, Sir. So I think his wife did' said I dryly, because it was evident to me. Right, she didn't kill him with her own hands; yet she was part of it.

'His wife?' Laverton started to laugh. 'Nonsense. She was in France when Russo died. This is a very stupid idea even for you, Mr Morgan. She called her husband and they talked to each other at 9 pm before the guy took a hot bath. We have the phone call list. 45 seconds. Mrs Russo told me that was a strange conversation. I quote: *he asked me how do you do, then he told me how much he loved me and said goodbye.* The woman understood that was a farewell when the police announced Russo's death. She had a bad feeling all night and she was right. Incidentally, Mrs Russo mentioned her husband repeatedly threatened to do so… Mrs Russo is so attractive; it isn't surprising that her husband chose death, not the life without her. It's simple' explained Laverton as if it were merely a difficult mathematical example.

No, a murder never is simple—I thought, but I didn't reply.

'I haven't any time… Dismissed' Laverton pointed to the door.

'You're wrong, Sir. She did it. I don't know how, but she did it, I'm sure.' That was my last attempt.

'Don't be ridiculous! *Means, motive and opportunity* that thesis was what we learnt. What is the motivation, Mr Morgan? Russo's belongings are worth about £800. Mrs Russo has hundreds of thousands of pounds… However, you have nothing, only a book and some delusions. Dismissed—I said. I'm terribly busy. And I'll tell you one more thing, Mr Morgan. If your freak show comes back again, I won't be so polite.'

There was nothing to do, I stood up and slammed Laverton's office door behind me—with respect of course. I wasn't the angry cause of his attitude, but rather because he was right. I didn't have a motivation.

'Idiot!' I murmured. Yes, I was an idiot to think Laverton would have been willing to help.

I grimaced as I had to explain that situation to Mrs Alford and Mr Brown. I waved to them and I headed outside when I bumped into somebody, and a cup of tea spilt on my dark suit. It was Heather O'Neil.

'Terrible sorry, Mr M' she excused herself. 'I'll bring a towel soon'

'It's nothing, don't worry about it' answered I.

Heather O'Neil was fast, a few seconds later she wiped my suit with a beige towel and slipped something into my pocket.

'O'Neil, you're so clumsy. Bring me another tea now!' ordered Laverton, who had ventured out of his office.

'Yes, Sir!' Heather replied quickly.

'You cannot say anything. We heard all of the words' said Mrs Alford while we went down the stairs. 'That man reminds me my second husband. He was smug and drama queen, for that reason it had been a short marriage of only two months.'

'Sickening' added Mr Brown.

If they would know how much!

'That phone call is fake' continued Mrs Alford. 'They could have discussed anything. Mr Russo is dead; we will never know the truth.'

I totally agreed.

'However, Laverton was right about one thing' noted I a few seconds later.

'What do you mean?' asked Mrs Alford.

'The motivation. I don't know what was Mrs Russo's motivation' responded I thoughtfully. 'Perhaps tomorrow we'll be wiser.'

'Good idea! Let's think about it' suggested Mr Brown. 'I will write down everything that comes to my mind.'

That was the bitter end of our unsuccessful and brief visit to the police station... Later, when I was alone, I checked my special message which Heather O'Neil had written on a yellow note paper: *at 8 pm in the Dublin.*

———

The *Dublin* was an Irish pub and the police's headquarters—I mean, the policemen's and retired ones' too. Jim Burton, the counter—an ex-cop—was a good-humoured fellow; however, three years ago his right knee had been shot, and since, half of it was made by platinum. Jim Burton's right knee had become perfect forecast weather, especially cold and rainy days. There usually was a good company in the *Dublin*, because that was a *Laverton-free* area.

I arrived at 7:45 pm.

'Morgan!' waved Burton when I entered. 'You haven't shown your face for a long time. I understand why: not a pretty sight.'

'Thanks! Tell me some interesting thing *what* I don't know, Jim.'

'With pleasure' bowed he. 'Laverton says, you're in rehab now.'

'It's nice. Alcohol or drugs?'

'Both of them' Jim Burton grinned at me with his incomplete set of teeth.

'Then I want a tonic water and an ale' ordered I.

'Oh! You have a guest. A pretty girl, isn't it? A redhead, I think' he pointed to the entrance.

Heather O'Neil stood there and looked around. She arrived early too.

A few minutes later we sat at a table in the back.

'Do you still remember what my favourite is?' Heather smiled and then blushed.

I nodded.

'The Superintendent Laverton said that you...'

'I know. They also talk about at the counter.'

There was a pause. I decided to let Heather start to speak. She hesitated a little bit and then leaned closer.

'You're interesting in the Russo case, right?' whispered she.

I nodded again.

'You have to see this, Mr Morgan.' She took some carefully folded papers out of her bag: a document in French and a copy of an old sketchbook's page. There was a type of medieval siege tower plan with a detailed description. It was drawn with brownish ink.

'Help me, please. My French is so weak' asked I. That document mentioned some drawings of da Vinci if I understood well, but I wasn't sure.

'This is an official certification which declares, the attached da Vinci sketch is a fake. A lesser-known French art historian stated that' explained Heather O'Neil. 'Laverton told you something about the motivation. I think this was the motivation.'

'This certification?'

Heather looked at me in amazement, suddenly her eyes lit up.

'Sorry. I forget the most important information fact. A few years ago another da Vinci drawing study was sold for £8 million… *Head of a bear…*'

I tried to put together what I knew.

'You mean Mr Russo had this sketch' I showed the copy.

'Exactly, Mr M. The certificate was sent by Russo's wife yesterday. Russo rented a safe for this sketch' added Heather. 'Last Friday she cancelled the rental and took the sketch to France.'

'With judicial permission of course.'

'Correct.'

It was understandable. Mrs Russo had to explain why she was cancelled the safe's rental.

'This lesser-known fellow wrote a certification because they paid for it… Later, when they put up the sketch for auction. If someone from—for example—Christie's states differently, who will care what this fellow wrote earlier… £8 million is a very good motivation' declared I. 'Therefore worth killing… But why now?' I turned to Heather.

'Maybe Russo wanted to change his will.'

'That's logical… Do you know who Mrs Russo's new boyfriend is? Russo's students talked about him. He's a French businessman having an electronics company.'

'No, sorry. I mean, not yet, but I'll find out by tomorrow... It's strange. Mrs Russo didn't mention her French friend when Laverton interrogated her.'

No coincidence.

'And what about your exam?'

'I don't have time, I'm so busy. Tea and cake, you know' replied Heather O'Neil cheerfully. 'We miss you very much' added she sadly. 'I hope you will come back.'

There was not much chance of that.

'And you. What are you doing now?'

'I was a portrait model in Mr Russo's art class. He found my face very unique' I joked.

'I see. That was why you started to investigate, wasn't that?'

'Yes. The suicide does not fit Mr Russo's psychological character.'

'Laverton would say that you're involved in this case, and he would exclude you... We can also say, he has already excluded you...' reflected Heather.

Twenty minutes later, we were walking on the street. I decided to accompany Heather home. Suddenly somebody pushed me up.

'Sorry' he murmured and fled.

I felt the stabbing. I stopped right away. I touched my stomach, and my palm was red with blood.

'Jesus!' cried Heather. 'You have to stop the bleeding. Don't worry, Mr Morgan...'

She dragged me somewhere. I heard her voice and perhaps Jim Burton said something...

EIGHT

WHEN I WOKE up, I saw Crachet head nurse watching my infusion.

'Good morning, Chief... Sorry, Mr Morgan!' she smiled at me very gently.

Usually, Crachet was like a drill sergeant. Except with the dying patients. So that was not a good omen.

I wanted to reply to her, but I couldn't speak.

'You're very weak, lost a lot of blood' explicated she. 'I'll give you something to help you sleep again.'

I noticed a syringe in her hand, and she injected some colourless liquid into my left arm.

'Good boy' said her.

Next time Heather O'Neil stood by my bed with Mr Brown and Mrs Alford.

'How are you, Mr Morgan?' Heather kissed my face.

'We were very worried about you' Mrs Alford noted leaning over me.

'I made muffins for you. Do not eat the hospital food. It's terrible, trust me' that was Mr Brown perhaps. He showed an elegant box. 'With sour cherry. I remember that you like it.'

Eat? I was glad to keep my eyes open.

'He's so pale' whispered Mrs Alford to Mr Brown.

I wanted to thank them, but not a single sound came out of my throat. Then Crachet head nurse arrived and ordered everyone out of the room.

It could have been at night. Doctor Robertson sat next to me.

'You almost ended up on my table, Morgan' started he. 'That nice redhead saved your life. By the way you and her…?'

I shook my head.

'I don't understand. I wanted to invite her, still, she said no… Never mind. The most important thing is that you do not eat the hospital food. I'll bring you some sandwiches from the canteen, right?'

I nodded.

'Although I see, you have this and that.'

I carefully turned right. While I slept, my supply had increased. There were Mr Brown's muffins, a big box of handmade Belgian chocolate, oranges, apples and two packets of Italian breadsticks.

'May I?' asked Robertson politely.

Of course.

The next few days passed like that. I didn't remember too much, and what I did, could have been a dream. Little had changed; fewer and fewer tubes were hanging out of me, and more and more food was on my bedside table. I received a teddy bear dressed as Bobby and a children's drawing with *We wish you well, Mr Morgan! The Simpsons* text—different colour and size letters. Those kids created something between *Pat the Postman* and *Paddington* in police uniform. I liked it.

Then one morning Crachet head nurse rushed in as a cavalry charge and ripped the blanket off me.

'Morning, Mr Morgan! Don't be lazy.'

She didn't leave much time, withdrew my catheter lightning fast, and then my voice came back.

'Don't be childish!' she ordered me, after that she dragged me to the bathroom.

I was made to take a shower, all while I saw the stars in pain. When I finished, she ordered me back in the bed. A few minutes later an army of doctors arrived. I was an educational material. They touched and pushed me, and changed my bandage while examining my wound. I just lay there like a wax figure of Madame Tussauds. They spoke in medical Latin, I didn't understand a single word. Afterwards, my miseries continued—not physically, mentally—because my ex-wife and her new husband visited me. Ruth gave another box of Belgian chocolate—the first one I had presented to Crachet head nurse, and I suspected this to be the second box's fate.

'Oh, Sean!' Ruth looked at me with pity.

Honestly, of the two of us, it was me, for whom the situation was more uncomfortable.

'Don't worry, Ruth, just the usual' I tried to smile.

'You're skin and bones' said she.

'You know me; I was never a big eater.'

A teardrop flowed down her face.

'Come on, darling. Let him rest' whispered the new husband.

Hey! I was her first man, not you... pal!... Never mind. It was my moment, but he had stolen it.

'You're right, Steve' approved Ruth. 'Take care, Sean!' She blew a kiss and went away.

That was worse than the catheter.

■—■—■—■□■—■—■—■

I slowly started to come back to the reality. I listened to the noises filtering in from the corridor. One of them was very familiar: a male voice who greeted everyone who passed by him. That was Sergeant Pulasky, an old hand. So I was guarded.

There was lunchtime. I was so hungry and could have eaten everything, but fortunately Mr Brown came with several boxes.

'I was in a hurry to get here on time' explained he. 'Crachet head nurse said that you're better and have already woken up. Wonderful!' I have always admired his enthu-siasm. 'This is a delicious soup from my favourite French restaurant, especially for you, Mr Morgan.'

I didn't pay much attention to the etiquette; I quickly scooped it all up.

'Roast duck with steamed vegetables. You can eat it cold too' continued Brown.

I didn't wait for it to cool down, I finished off. When Mrs Alford entered, I was eating the dessert—a great slice of apple cake.

'Did he eat everything?' asked she as a worried mother.

'He did' answered Brown proudly, *my father*.

'Right. Now for the coffee.' She pulled out a huge thermos from her large handbag and three cups, spoons, sugar and a little bottle of cream. 'This is my favourite: with vanilla flavour.'

She served us the coffee. I started to feel more human again.

'You look better, Mr Morgan' said Mrs Alford. 'We were worried about you, I mean: Mr Brown, Heather and me. She's a lovely girl, isn't she?' Mrs Alford winked at me. She started again.

'Constable O'Neil is a smart girl, yes' replied I quickly. Usually, I like to talk about Heather O'Neil, but at that moment I had many questions. 'What day it is today?'

'Monday' responded Mr Brown.

I had wasted a week.

'A lot of things have happened while you've been here' continued he, and turned to Mrs Alford.

'Heather sent you a message: she will visit after her shift. And asked us to show you' she handed me a newspaper. 'Sixth page.'

In the middle, there was a great colour picture. The Superintendent Laverton stood in front of my bed with a serious face. I was behind him, unconsciously and full of tubes, like a very bizarre decoration. What about my rights? What about them? Nothing. I haven't any rights.

Laverton said in the newspaper, that the attack could relate to one of my previous cases. The whole police force had worked day and night to catch that person. I translate for you: *Laverton has no idea and the suspect went far, they will never catch him.*

'Nice pic' noted I. 'Anything else?'

'Mr Russo's body was cremated, he'll be buried in France' listed Mrs Alford. 'We held a little reunion on Friday and made a memorial corner in the classroom. There are his ochre coat, his brushes, oil paint, easel and palette. One of his students painted a portrait about him, and Mr Brown brought an ebony bookcase for Mr Russo's stuff. You'll have to see it, Mr Morgan, if you leave this terrible place.'

I wasn't surprised by the cremation. That was the final step of Mrs Russo's plan. We don't have the body, no exhumation, that's all.

I knew well, that my attacker was the same person who murdered Mr Russo. He liked to use a knife, an ex-soldier or a mercenary. He was professional and they paid him well. I remembered well the £8 million sketch too. Maybe they were content to put me to bed for a few weeks. However, I was careful, and I didn't speak about Mr Russo's legacy.

'What do you think, Mr Morgan?' questioned Mrs Alford.

'Merry widow.'

'Cruel woman' added Mr Brown.

I sipped from my coffee thoughtfully.

'Oh, Mr Morgan! You owe me' smiled Mrs Alford mysteriously.

'I beg your pardon…'

'I wanted to finish your portrait' explained she. 'You're very inspiring.'

'Really?' I was hoping she was joking.

'Really. You know, Mr Morgan, I don't like the incomplete work.'

I sipped my coffee again instead of an answer.

❚—❚—❚—❚▢❚—❚—❚—❚

Robertson came to see me in the afternoon. He ate the rest of the apple cake and brought four homemade cucumber sandwiches instead. I think he had exchanged them for something else earlier.

'Do you know anything about Russo's cremation?'

Robertson swallowed what was in his mouth.

'Strange thing' answered he. 'The old mummy was surprised yet. Laverton closed the case last Monday…'

The old mummy was Professor Grant, the head of the morgue.

'According to the original plan, the undertaker would take the body on Wednesday' explicated Robertson. 'After that, they came on Monday evening. You can imagine. Grant was seething with rage. He cried: *the rule is the rule; Monday isn't Wednesday and get out.* Twenty minutes later his phone rang. It was Judge McGowan. The undertakers came back and took the body away. Grant has been swearing ever since. *This is a serious violation of the hospital rules* he imitated the Professor's voice. '*Scandalous!*

Professor Grant was right: there were many rule violations in that case. How interesting, that didn't bother Laverton or the Judge.

Robertson stuffed a large piece of apple cake into his mouth.

'That nice ginger… she comes to see you every day. I think she loves you, Morgan' he spoke, chewed and grinned at once.

■—■—■—■□■—■—■—■

If Laverton wanted, Heather O'Neil's shift would end at 6 pm. Heather was late, thus I assumed Laverton had ordered overtime. When I heard her voice, it was 8:30 pm.

'Evening, Mr Morgan! Mr Brown told me that you finally got out of bed.' She entered the room.

'Good evening, Constable O'Neil!' I greeted her restrainedly; however, I was curious to know about what she had investigated.

'I'll give you some shortbread. His Majesty likes it—the ad said so' Heather smiled at me. Shortly after, she took a seat on a small stool. 'His name is Jean-Michel Allard and has no files at French Police, nor Scotland Yard. He's clean.'

'Did you check him at the Interpol?'

'No, Sir. I don't have access.'

But I had—more precisely, I had received fourteen months ago, and I hoped, it was still usable.

'I need a notebook or something similar' noted I.

Heather conjured up a small silver-grey laptop from his backpack. Perfect!

I opened Interpol's special website; user name, and password, and I was on. Searching: Jean-Michel Allard—that was a beautiful French name, pretty. His original was Jan Adamec, not typical just in Slovakia. Adamec had a criminal record: GBH—grievous bodily harm—and CCW—carrying a concealed weapon. In the last few years, he was arrested twice on charges of arms smuggling, but they had no evidence. That was Mrs Russo's new boyfriend. Exciting and dangerous. And that man had a da Vinci sketch worth £8 million. Not very encouraging.

NINE

THEY DIDN'T TORTURE me the next morning—I mean doctors, nurses or visitors. After my modest breakfast, I lazed in my bed and stared at the ceiling. A fat, dark brown spider walked across above me. I hoped it wouldn't fall on my chest. Finally, it disappeared in a thin gap between two plasterboards. I was bored because my phone was still in the lab by order of the Superintendent Laverton. Thus I stared at the ceiling.

After 10 pm, Robertson visited me. He brought a thick book: *The History of Pathology*. The last Professor had left in the morgue and the new one wanted to throw it in the trash. Robertson had saved it—until that moment he hidden it in his desk drawer. Six hundred and eighty-two pages. It kept me busy for a while. I started to read immediately... I confess that my knowledge of that theme had been incomplete—I could change that. I was reading the first chapter—the foreword lasted thirty-two pages and talked about nothing—when I heard a strange sound.

'No one can enter while I'm here' commanded a firm voice, Superintendent Laverton, himself.

I closed the book quickly and slipped it under my blanket.

'Here is the victim' noted Laverton grinning, when he entered. 'Hopefully you rested enough, Mr Morgan, and you're capable of answering my questions.'

I do my best.

Laverton snapped his finger to his Sergeant, who placed a chair next to my bed.

'So, Mr Morgan, according to Constable O'Neil's report, she and you walking on the street. Right?'

'I don't remember well, Sir… We met in the *Dublin*, drank something and after I offered to accompany her… Somebody pushed me and then my palm was bloody. Constable O'Neil cried out. That was the last thing that I can recall, Sir' I said in an official tone.

'I see… Why did you meet there?'

'I wanted to speak to her.'

'Why?'

I had to lie, but it would not seem incredible.

'Because I'm interested in her career, in her future' I responded. 'I wanted give some advice to her.'

'At your age, Mr Morgan? You would be her father. Disgusting' grimaced Laverton. *Poor man, he cannot imagine any other relationship between a woman and a man.*

Earlier, I had the desire to tell Laverton the truth, but at that moment it was gone.

'I don't care. This is your business…' continued he. 'Would you like to say something else?'

I shook my head.

'Exactly as I thought. You're useless' he remarked disapprovingly, and for several long minutes he detailed that I was just wasting his time.

■–■–■–■□■–■–■–■

Lunch with my new parents: Mrs Alford and Mr Brown, and a big sleep. I had eaten too much and I dreamed all kinds of things. Laverton was also in it. He came into the room and started to shout. *Come on, get up! Can you hear me?...*

'Can you hear me? Wake up!' That was no longer Laverton.

I opened my eyes, and I saw a black guy in an elegant suit.

'Wake up, *Monsieur* Morgan. Can you hear me?'

Ha wasn't alone, was accompanied by three others.

'Yes, I can hear you, Sir' I spoke suspiciously. 'Who are you?'

He knew my name, but I had never seen him before.

'Alex Dubois, Interpol. You hacked into our system.'

I quickly sat up in bed.

'That's not true, Sir. I have a legal password. I got it from your officer.'

'Yes, we know that. However, you aren't a police officer any more, thus you don't have permission to use it.'

Damn! He caught me.

'Sorry, Sir. I'll accept the consequences.'

'*Eh, bien!* he waved his hand in annoyance. 'I don't really care. Rather, tell me, why you checked Jan Adamec's file.'

I felt we had similar areas of interest. If I was wrong, he could think the explosion drove me crazy. I told him my theory about Mr Russo's treasure, his wife and her new boyfriend.

'A da Vinci sketch?' asked Dubois laughing. '*C'est un idiot*' he said to his fellow.

My French was weak—as I mentioned before—, still, I understood perfectly.

'Your permission is cancelled. *Comprenez, crétin?*' he turned away, murmured something in French and hurried with his silent company.

My test was successful. I could imagine an ordinary police officer's reaction. How lucky I hadn't shared it with anyone else!

∎–∎–∎–∎▫∎–∎–∎–∎

Heather O'Neil arrived after 9 pm. She looked tired and moody. She gave me my *Dorian Gray* as I had requested before. It was a more exciting read than the *The History of Pathology*: the life and work of many doctors somehow did not inspire me.

'Sorry for my late, Mr Morgan. I had a terrible day' explicated she.

'Don't mention it. I'm betting for Laverton.'

'How did you know?' wondered Heather.

'He interrogated me, and finally, he stated I was an unusable victim and witness in one.'

'He also talked to me.' She hesitated a few seconds then she started to speak. 'He ordered me to his office. I was there about for half an hour. He thinks you are a very manipulative person, a psychopath. That I'd better avoid you. After that, he called my mother… I know that because my mother called me. So he told my mother that you wanted to seduce me. You can imagine! If I didn't stop her, she would already be organizing the wedding. You know, Mr Morgan, my mother likes you… By the way, I like you, but I don't love…' She looked at me waiting. 'You're the only one who cares about me…'

I was a little relieved, to be honest.

'Don't worry; I have no intention of seducing you… I care about you, yes, because I think you are destined for more than serving tea and biscuits.' I answered.

Heather sighed.

'Thank God!' smiled she, then suddenly she looked scared. 'Poor mother… how can I tell her?'

'Maybe you can wait…'

'You're right. I'll wait.'

'Speaking of honest confessions…' continued I 'The Interpol was here. A black guy who's named Alex Dubois. He wasn't too happy and cancelled my permission. I suspected he was hunting for Mrs Russo's friend, however, he wasn't interested in my theory.'

'If you want, I'll check out that Dubois' offered Heather.

'Do you think it makes sense?'

'Yes, I think so' nodded she. 'Maybe I'll find something.'

There was no other direction to go. Why not?

Heather promised to visit me later. Finally, I was alone with *Dorian Gray*.

■—■—■—■□■—■—■—■

I fell asleep. In the middle of the last chapter, I fell asleep with the book in my lap. I'd been yawing since Heather O'Neil left. It was a wonder I had got that far in reading.

'Wake up, Morgan!' That was Dubois again. I was sure it was a dream.

I opened my eyes, and tried to understand what he was talking about. It wasn't so simple because he spoke in French.

'I beg your pardon?' I interrupted when I had completely lost the tread. It was a very real dream and I wanted to understand him.

'Mrs Russo and Adamec are dead. His schooner exploded fourteen hours ago' repeated Dubois in English.

I became alert at once. I sat up in my bed.

'What are you talking about?'

'The Saint-Tropez Police called me. They know we observe Jan Adamec' responded Dubois. 'Adamec's boat exploded near the port. Dozens of witnesses saw when Adamec and the woman boarded the schooner. One of them, another ship-owner, spoke to them about the weather, and then they sailed out. A few minutes later the witnesses heard a great explosion. Adamec's boat, what was left of it, was on fire. The Police found two charred corpses.'

I was shocked. I needed a few minutes to think.

'Who identified the bodies?' asked I. That accident was suspicious. There were many witnesses, an explosion near to the port, so quick and so spectacular.

'They found some DNA samples of Adamec and Mrs Russo, and we have their fresh dental files. Adamec and Mrs Russo were at the dentist last month... There was a numbered Omega watch on Adamec's arm—I checked it, he bought it six months ago. The woman wore a necklace, bracelet and rings—they can be easily identified from the photos. There was Adamec's phone... Wait a minute! You know something, don't you?' Dubois caught my hospital gown, he looked pretty hot. 'Speak!'

He started to pull me, and my book fell on the floor.

'I don't know more than you do' I answered and picked *Dorian Gay*, its spine was broken. It automatically opened at the end of the novel. 'In fact, you are the one who knows more.'

Dubois told me something, but I didn't listen to him because I read the last sentence of *Dorian Gray*: *It was not till they had examined the rings that they recognized who it was.*

Rings... dental files... DNA... identified... At that moment, I understood.

'Morgan!' cried Dubois. 'Are you right?'

'Dentist... That was the first time, when Adamec was there, right?'

'*Quoi?*'

'It's very simple' I started my explanation. 'Adamec wanted to disappear and start a new life with a new identity. Now he has a £8 million sketch... He planned it all well in advance. The watch and the jewellery, the dentist... there were the requisites of identification. Adamec paid a couple who went to the dentist using their names. After then, Adamec killed them. He needed the bodies. DNA... We know well how easy it is to place. Adamec and Mrs Russo arrived at the port, talked to somebody, boarded and sailed out. The bodies were already on the board. There are many witnesses—you said. It was a trick.'

Dubois laughed at me, suddenly he was gloomy.

'If you're right...'

'If I'm right, the sketch will be released soon...'

Dubois frowned.

'But if you're wrong...'

'If I'm wrong... Adamec is dead. You have nothing to lose... Find Constable Heather O'Neil directly and tell her it was me who sent you. The Constable has a copy of the sketch and a fake certification. She'll help you. You should settle for double murder instead of charges of arms smuggling. If you find the missing couple and their connection with Adamec, you'll have your evidence too.'

Dubois looked at me so suspiciously, then he hurried away.

TEN

HEATHER TOLD ME that Dubois had visited her that night. Since then it's been quiet—at least as far as Dubois is concerned, but Laverton was actively involved in my life; he thoroughly reorganized. For example, he suggested sending me to a therapy group where they deal with abused victims. *Thank you so much.* Thus I spent my time every Friday evening with my new fellows. I didn't feel like a victim, but it didn't matter. Mrs Alford and Mr Brown accompanied me—of course. They said *I cannot recognize my victimization because of trauma.*

That Friday evening—I had left my hospital bed two weeks ago—the therapist, Doctor Hughes, made me speak about my misery. He was a stubborn guy and very irritating. He wasn't satisfied with the facts, and he wanted to know how I felt. Nonsense! I felt nothing. They stabbed me, and I investigated who paid for it. That was enough for me. So why not for him? He tortured me for twenty minutes—it seemed to me more like two hours.

'I think, you are buried so deep in your pain, Sean' Doctor Hughes summed up his opinion. 'We will need a long time. I suggest doubling the length of your therapy.'

Great! Six months—an eternity.

I wasn't in a good mood. Mr Brown answered with his usual enthusiasm:

'Maybe Superintendent Laverton wants to help you.'

Does Laverton want to help me? That did not make me happier.

When I went out onto the street, I saw Dubois. He was standing next to an SUV, and unlike me, he seemed very cheerful.

'*Bonsoir, Monsieur* Morgan!' waved he. 'May I invite you for dinner?'

'This guy is from the Interpol, sorry. I have to go with him.' I turned to Mr Brown and briefly explained the situation.

'Don't worry, Mr Morgan. Duty calls you...' smiled Brown.

'Perhaps you can introduce us to this elegant gentleman' noted Mrs Alford while adjusting her dress.

Yes, I did it.

A few minutes later I sat in the Interpol's SUV *face à face* Dubois.

'I don't like your *cuisine*...' started he. 'And you could probably guess I don't want to eat. I just want to talk to you.'

I nodded, and I was glad to not eat for example snails or frogs.

'We caught Adamec… dead, not alive' he continued. 'An art expert of Sotheby's called us. Adamec brought the da Vinci sketch there—you were right. We followed him… I also found a young couple: the husband worked in Adamec's company as an electrical engineer. They went to that dentist—we searched their previous dental files. Moreover, Adamec transferred all of the money from their bank account to the Cayman Islands, exactly like from his company's account—that was ten minutes after his spectacular death.'

This dead man clings to his possessions.

'I think' said Dubois 'Adamec calculated when we realized the exchange and the bank transfers, it would be too late.'

'It seemed he thought everything' nodded I.

'Not quite… Although that is also true if we hadn't known Russo's da Vinci sketch, he would have gotten away with it all, but he was too greedy. We followed him and at the convenient moment, we prepared for his arrest. It began officially but ended in a shootout. Adamec was the one who started shooting. We broke into his house… the woman was already dead; Adamec shot her in the head. He didn't give in easily; one of my men was injured. Finally, my best sniper neutralised him. The bitter end, but we have his laptop and we have already have arrested nine people.'

'Congratulations.'

'Thank you, *Monsieur* Morgan…' said he. 'But I don't know what I do with this sketch. Maybe I can attach it as evidence… or you have a better proposal, don't you?'

Yes, I do.

'Russo's art school would be grateful, I think.'

'Right' Dubois agreed. 'I was sure you told me that thus I called the manager yesterday. It is a pleasure working with you, Mr Morgan… and I restored your access. Feel free to read our files; it's just good for me.'

I believe that!

∎—∎—∎—∎▢∎—∎—∎—∎

I decided my investigative company had a right to know the dramatic finale. The next day I invited Heather, Mrs Alford and Mr Brown to dinner. I'm not a good cook, but I can prepare frozen food or heat something from the fridge and I'm a great master at ordering. Finally, I chose Mrs and Mr Bianchi's sandwiches and a bottle of Chianti—in memory of Mr Russo.

Heather O'Neil arrived first—I asked her to come earlier because there were certain details I wanted to share just with her. Heather listened excitedly to my unofficial report.

'You know what's the best part, Mr M?' asked she cheerfully.

'I think it's that the art school acquired Russo's legacy' I replied as I thought it.

'No! The best part is, Laverton doesn't know anything about is' Heather started to laugh.

I liked that too and I was able to pay for the hospital report with the great colour picture.

Suddenly somebody rang. Those were Mrs Alford with a bottle of Martini Asti—in a particularly conservative costume without giant flowers—and Mr Brown wearing his favourite pink checkered sweater and with Tiramisu—I had suspected he would make some delicious Italian cake.

After my guests took a seat I served the sandwiches with Chianti. Yes, I know that was a surprising pairing, but appropriate for the occasion. Then I started my monologue.

'What a terrible story!' said Mrs Alford a few minutes later. 'Although… divine judgement I think.'

'*Judicium divinum*' noticed Mr Brown.

Probably, because Laverton couldn't do it justice.

Blasted Book Club

ONE

'*THIS BRILLIANT, LOVING boy, who calls me father in his inno-cence...*' Mrs Alford read loud, but suddenly her voice cracked, and she wiped away a giant teardrop on her face. A few seconds later, she continued to read very slowly, stuttering.

Honestly, I didn't understand that situation: why she experienced that text so much. Thus, I stared intently at my book so that the others didn't notice my insensitivity. It was too dangerous in such a place like this—punctually in such a circle like this.

Two months ago, Doctor Hughes gave me a certificate of completion, which had a rigid criterion: I had to maintain a social life. It was very hard for me, indeed, because I'm not a typical partygoer. As if Doctor Hughes hadn't trusted me enough, he had sent me to Miss Evans' book club. Doctor Hughes and Miss Evans had been classmates in Oxford many years ago and friends currently—that was my bad luck. In summary, every Wednesday afternoon, I had to go to Miss Emily Evans' bookshop, where the book club met. Miss Evans was a grey-haired, thin older woman—like a Gothic vampire lady who hadn't drunk blood for a long time. I was sure there were a lot of books in her head, more than in her bookshop. She watched me sternly, a little suspiciously if I were one of the bad students—you have to know that my fixed place, my chair, stood opposite her.

Fortunately, I wasn't alone. Mrs Alford and Mr Brown accompanied me there. We became friends after our special investigation, and both of them shared a love for literature. For example, Mr Brown had written a few poems when he was a young boy—they're so good, I think.

When we joined that club, the others had already read the first half of the actual book, yet we quickly made up for the lost ground.

That evening was the last meeting of that novel, and Miss Evans wanted to know what our favourite part was. I tried to choose something neutral, something from Persia, and I hoped Miss Evans forgot about me.

Yes, I hoped it was because we were nine. I mean, there were more than eight enthusiastic members of this *beautiful* club—and me, who was less passionate. First, Mrs Alford, my unofficial stepmother and friend—not more than that—, who always wore a colourful dress with giant flowers, had a striking personality. Mrs Alford, also Sophia, was a sensitive and determined woman: you could not contradict her, but she could tear some romantic stories. She was on my left side.

Second, my unofficial stepfather, Mr Cecil Brown. He was an empathetic man and an excellent baker—he regularly gave different types of cakes in our book club. When I saw him the first time, he was wearing a pink checkered sweater, but I knew he had that piece of clothing in the entire colour palette. That evening, he wore a sea blue one with an apple green shirt—that was his design. Next to him, Mr John Cartwright sat another grey-haired fellow, who loved the hand-sewn Italian fashion and Mr Brown's cakes—so much. By the way, Mr Cartwright was an officer—I think his work was so dull, not him. Two weeks ago, for example, he mentioned that he had collected antique books, such as Lord Byron's first publication.

Then, there was Lucy Taylor, a timid girl with long blond hair full of pimples and inhibitions. I think she liked the handsome and hectic *Vronsky* type—using a literary example from *Anna Karenina*—but I'm afraid she had to settle for the predictable *Levin*.

As I mentioned earlier, Miss Evans and I sat face-to-face, like two Siamese fighting fish, but that analogy was incorrect. Miss Bluestocking Evans was tendentious and warlike; nevertheless, I tried to hide behind my book—perhaps that was my fault—and I always had to answer her questions. Yes, I had to respond because she started her sentence like that: 'Sean, what do you think…'

Sorry, I've strayed a bit from the topic. So… continuing the presentation of our little book club, on my right side, there were two friendly and quiet housewives: Judith Lynch and Marthe Laroche. Mrs Lynch adored romance novels; her favourite was Jane Austin's complete works, and he read every book in which there was only a tiny bit of love. She also looked at life through these rosy glasses. As you understand her philosophy, you must know that Mrs Lynch thought every arrogant, selfish man was *Mr Darcy*. On the contrary, Mrs Laroche was a reasonable woman who knew well when to dream and when to change a diaper. These Wednesday afternoons were her dream time.

Finally, there was an extraordinary young couple. Mr and Mrs Singh: Aryan and Preeti. At first, I thought there were two literature students. They watched everything like in the school, and they took notes; perhaps they used that club for their thesis. Thereafter, I checked them on the web, and what I found? Mr Singh had written half a dozen romance novels under the pseudonym Marguerite White, and his wife was an economist. Queer. Mr Singh and his smart *rib* calculated that they conducted market research in our club. Perhaps Mr Singh hoped to get closer to his female readers' hearts if he wrote to their taste. What a scientific method!

'This brilliant, loving boy, who calls me father in his innocence...' Mrs Alford read loud, but suddenly her voice cracked... When she finished the lecture, she looked up with tearful eyes. 'This was the most beautiful part of the last chapter', noticed she.

'Thank you, Sophia' said Miss Evans. 'I think you're interested in the father-son relationship, aren't you?'

'You're right, Emily. At the end of the story, it is essential to me. I see that the count's character changed too, and he became a much more serious person' explained she.

John Cartwright and Mr Brown nodded while Mrs Lynch wiped away her tears. Aryan Singh glanced at his wife and quickly wrote something.

'I'm very curious. What do you think, Sean.' Miss Evans stared straight at me behind her large-rimmed glasses.

'It's very effective... I mean impressive' I stammered, and I was hoping that would be enough.

'No, Sean. I want to know what you think.' Miss Evans was cruel.

It was like an execution—but I think about it, it is much faster.

'Honestly' she added.

I was sure she would let me go only if I told the truth. Honestly? Right.

'So... The main character... I mean the protagonist...'

'Yes?'

'I think that man is a cold-blooded serial killer who wants to possess that girl and can destroy everyone and everything. He's a sociopath. That girl should be grateful not to get married to him,' I answered, but they didn't applaud me.

There was a tense silence. Lucy Taylor—that timid young woman—could have killed me by her eyes.

'Sean, I think you cannot leave your earlier life, your profession, and you're unable to see the story from a different perspective' noted Miss Evans. 'Do you know that you treat one of the most romantic love story's characters like a criminal? You degrade the *Phantom of the Opera* to a sociopath. It's so sad... for you.'

'You have no imagination!' cried Lucy Taylor angrily. 'Why did you come here? How can you understand such a great man like *Eric?*'

'Miss Taylor, believe me, I tried to understand your loved character, but he unquestionably is a serial killer' I tried to reason.

'Self-defense!'

'So many times? Nonsense! I calculated how many people were killed by him' I showed her my notes because I did a thorough job.

Mr Brown started to laugh. For some reason, he found it funny that I kept records of the *Phantom*'s victims.

'Miss Taylor, please forgive Mr Morgan! He's an excellent police officer, but...' he wanted to help me but in vain.

'A police officer?' Miss Taylor asked in surprise.

'An ex-police officer' nodded I.

'Fascist! Nazi!' shouted her.

Thank you! I'm a Nazi, yes, in such a case, but if there is a problem... Don't worry. I didn't take it to heart; I'm used to being told that. Many people dislike cops, especially idealistic young women.

'Despite how insensitive you are, Sean, you're able to whip up the feelings of others', stated Miss Evans dryly.

That's me, right.

'Does anyone have any comments on Sean's interpretation?' Miss Evans managed to keep her composure. She must have heard something more interesting than this.

'Yes, I have' said Marthe Laroche. 'We know well, Sean, that *Eric* was a sociopath serial killer, and in real life, I don't like him. I was a social worker, and I know what I'm talking about. But... but when I'm reading this book, I would like to hope he was a very sensible gentleman. Please, give me this illusion. And I might expect that's you who can understand him.'

Oh, my buried face again! Wonderful! I haven't lost my mind yet after a grenade pierced my left side. Otherwise, I thought Miss Evans enjoyed my torture.

'You know' continued Mrs Laroche 'Sean surely wants to read Stephen King's *Misery*.'

Miss Evans smiled, and I was extremely grateful to Mrs Laroche for that joke.

'I think so' told Miss Evans with sarcasm. 'Right. We have to choose the next reading. I have some suggestions...' She began to list the authors and titles.

I voted for what Mrs Alford and Mr Brown voted for. That would be okay, and it would be preferable if I left first and moved quickly. Anyway, we lost, and Stanley Phillips' love story won. Who the hell is that Stanley Phillips?

■—■—■—■□■—■—■—■

A few minutes later, I wandered through the streets—the Nazi epithet bothered me better than the comment about my face—after then, I saw a blue light subtitle: ONLY LONELY BAR. That was amusing but not unique. Perhaps I could finish that day with a double gin or something. I entered.

About my face briefly. My loved superior officer, Laverton, had sent me to check a scene, and then a grenade had explored next to me. The left side of my face and neck had burned a little bit. My ex-wife didn't like my new design, so we divorced. It wasn't a happy story, but I managed to survive.

In the bar, a very attractive young woman worked at the counter. I ordered my double gin and sat at a table in the twilight zone. After my first sip, I had to determine that my drink was watered down. Perhaps that was why there were no clients. I originally planned to spend a long time there, but finally, I decided to leave soon. I drank slowly, looked at the wall decoration—film noir photos in black and white—and I only had a few sips left when somebody came to my table.

'May I?' asked a female voice.

'Of course' I stood up quickly.

She smiled at me and took a seat.

'Thank you.'

'Not at all' answered I, and sat down again.

She wore an elegant black suit, black suitcase and black high-heeled shoes as she arrived from an evening funeral. She had a small silver… no!… rather white gold rose-shaped brooch with a white pearl, pearl earrings and necklace. Her makeup was solid, and she had a short, modern hairstyle. She drank a martini with a thin lemon slice. I had several guesses, from the luxury prostitute to the widow of a millionaire. I still couldn't realise which one was true. However, she had a white gold ring with diamonds on her left ring finger. I finally crossed the first option off my list.

'Does your drink also have a water taste?' asked she.

The alarm went off in my head, but I ignored it and ordered an unopened bottle of martini with two glasses.

TWO

Stella left at dawn. She didn't want her husband to find out about our *liaison*. That was completely understandable. Although, there was something that I didn't understand: why did I do such a crazy thing like that? I could have explained it by saying I drank a lot; even sober Stella's company was enjoyable.

I woke up at the usual time and began my morning run. Everything was simple and easy, and it was as if the whole world had changed. I should have known that I was in trouble.

So, when I had breakfast at Mr and Mrs Bianchi's coffee shop—delicious Italian sandwiches with ham and cheese—I noticed that my phone had been muted since the previous night. I adjusted it before the book club, and I forgot to reset it. I had nine missed calls and four messages. Mr Brown and Mrs Alford were worried about me so much. I called back Mrs Alford—ladies first. She had a very extreme idea: she thought if I watched *The Phantom of the Opera*—the musical, of course—I understand the story better. She had already brought three tickets for Friday evening, and she and her new boyfriend were taking me to the theatre in her Saab—I suspected she had a complex strategy to ensure I wouldn't miss the show. Thus, I had a Friday evening program—perfect.

After that, I called Mr Brown, who reminded me to go shopping. Precisely, we had previously agreed on where we would bring the next club book. Mr Brown was so attentive and didn't suggest Miss Evans' bookshop.

We met about 4 pm. Mr Brown wasn't alone; Mr Cartwright accompanied him.

'John said that is an excellent place.' Mr Brown was enthusiastic. No matter what happens, Mr Brown is always able to be enthusiastic.

'I hope we find something special' noted Mr Cartwright.

I nodded and followed them to the bookshop.

First, we searched for the required reading: a best-selling romance novel. After that, we started to explore the labyrinth. Mr Brown went towards the cookbooks, Mr Cartwright set up camp at the foreign language, and I got lost among the bookshelves. A few minutes later, I found myself next to the biography of Lord Nelson. A shelf displayed a critical edition of Lady Worsley's letters. A copy of the painting on the cover hung on the wall of my living room. The late Mr Russo had painted it and given it to me. I liked him and Lady Worsley as well. I took the book off the shelf and flipped through it. I thought there was something similar between Stella and Lady W. I guessed both of them had a foolish, selfish husband, and I was hoping I could help Stella. I decided to buy that book.

By the way, Stella and I had agreed not to look at each other—*Strangers in the Night* or *One Night Only* as you wish. We left it to fate what happens to us. So we may never see each other again or run into each other on the next street corner. Anything goes.

'Are you right, Sean?' Mr Brown approached me carrying many books.

'I'm fine' responded I very quickly.

'Do you find something?' he asked with curiosity.

I showed Lady Worsley's portrait to him.

'If I remember well, you have always been interested in this lady.'

'I think this is about something else' interrupted Mr Cartwright. It was a mystery where he was before. 'Our friend's in love.'

I hesitated.

'No… just I met somebody'

'Meet somebody. Gosh! It always starts like meet somebody' Mr Cartwright sighed.

I hoped he was wrong.

THREE

MRS ALFORD CALLED me several times on Friday, and the point was to choose something elegant suit. Elegant. That word reminded me of Stella—by the way, every word reminded me of Stella. So I took my black Hugo Boss out of the closet. I thought that with a black shirt and a black tie embroidered with silver threads—as if flames were rising. That could have been quite elegant.

Mrs Alford wore a burgundy velvet evening dress with many jewels and a hint of Chanel *Mademoiselle*—sorry, I'm just kidding—*No. 5*. She looked like she was going to the Olivier Awards. His actual boyfriend had a dinner jacket: black and white. The dress code was completed.

We sat in a box upstairs. Mrs Alford and her friend, Gérard, were in the first line, and I sank into the back seat. That seemed just right to me.

'I would be happy to lend it to you' she turned back to Mrs Alford and extended her opera glasses towards me. That meant I had to use it if I wanted to or not. That was a lovely piece: brass with mother-of-pearls inlay.

'You're kind, thank you' I said because I tried to be polite.

At first, I didn't know what to do with that; I checked the stage, the actors and actresses—nothing interesting—and after that, I examined the orchestra thoroughly. I noticed that one of the violinists had just one earring, and another one had a wig—it had slipped onto his head. I had a lot of fun like a child. I looked around among the audience, and then I noticed Stella. She sat in the other side box on the second level. She was wearing a dark dress that didn't cover her too much. Practically, I could see her bosom—especially if she leaned forward a little bit. Time passed quite slowly, even though I couldn't wait to meet finally.

After the end of the first act, Mrs Alford and her friend headed for the bars because she wanted her usual champagne. I suddenly stepped back, and then I hurried up to the second floor. Stella was there talking with an old couple. She looked at me, her eyes smiled.

'Excuse me' she said and went to the opposite direction, and I followed her.

She stopped and disappeared behind a small door. I went after her. There was a staff staircase. Stella ran down, me too. Finally, we were in a narrow storage room for cleaning equipment. Stella put her finger to my lips. I nodded, understanding well.

When I returned to our box, a masked man in a hooded cloak and a young woman in a traditional Spanish dress sang together about a *point of no return*. At that moment, I thought the same thing.

■—■—■—■□■—■—■—■

Don't forget, I'm an ex-police officer, and I always find the person who I'm looking for. It was true that we agreed, but we didn't promise.

I was crazy about Stella. I had to do something—I mean not just dreaming. Also, I had two starting points: the bar and the theatre. The second one was risky because of her husband, but the first one was a less known, dimly lit place. I started there—I secretly hoped I would find her.

There were water-tasted drinks and the same girl at the counter. I ordered a double gin, and I began a seemingly aimless conversation with her. I drank three rounds, but all I learned was that Stella had been there for the first time that night. I decided to continue the research the next day.

■—■—■—■□■—■—■—■

I couldn't sleep; I imagined our future, both the best and the worst versions. I preferred the best one, of course: we bought a lovely little house somewhere in Norfolk and lived quietly and happily. I knew it could never happen, but I liked it so much.

In the next three days, I visited those places where Stella might appear: galleries, concert halls, and restaurants. Mathematically, we had to meet sooner or later.

On Monday evening, I entered a French restaurant—*Chez Pierre* or something similar. After a lengthy discussion, I managed to get a table. While I walked towards my place,

I saw Stella. She wasn't alone. There were seven people at her table. She recognized me and nodded. I sat and waited. A few minutes later, Stella stood up and walked towards a back door. I followed her. That time, I found her in the corridor of the cold room.

'What do you think? Are you mad?' she asked with anger but whispering. 'My husband is here.'

'I've been looking for you...' I explained. I was confused.

'We agreed. Do you remember?'

'Yes, but...'

'Enough... I understand. Let's clear this up, Sean. It was good and exciting, but it's over, right?... It's over' repeated she.

'Stella...'

'Jesus! Did you take it seriously? Don't be ridiculous! You're not a child! Grow up! Or do you think that you and I...?' she laughed. 'That was only a play, nothing else.'

I could not speak.

'Please don't follow me, don't call me, right?'

She may have said something I don't remember, and I also don't remember how I left the building.

■—■—■—■□■—■—■—■

Lucy Taylor was wrong. I can imagine many fantastic things, like the life with Stella in the country yard, but I cannot imagine why Stella said those things. Perhaps she had many faces and wore many masks for each person or every situation. It was increasingly likely that she showed her true colours there, in the corridor, and she had a kind of routine, had a proven method. How many did she say in those sentences? Who knows? Only a play for her, that's all, but I think it's not so simple.

FOUR

ON TUESDAY AND Wednesday morning, I spent in self-pity. I ride an emotional roller coaster rarely, and I had no intention of spending more time on it than necessary—especially since I hadn't even opened the new book yet.

I was expecting a phone call saying the club was cancelling that afternoon. Instead, I received only a few reminder messages. Mr Brown had already read chapter five, and Mrs Alford wrote that the novel was excellent, so she finished it. I had to start it. Damned! That was bloody homework, and I felt that day wasn't mine.

I began that *excellent* reading… I tried to concentrate on the text—I swear—but failed to do so. I read the pages several times, in vain. I couldn't remember any of the words. That was not quite true… there was a sad woman and a handsome young man, somewhere they met, said goodbye and met again… I didn't understand. Never mind. Miss Evans could easily win.

■—■—■—■□■—■—■—■

Before the club, we—I mean Mrs Alford, Mr Brown, Mr Cartwright and I—usually gathered in Mrs Alford's favourite tea room. I was late; the others had already chatted happily. There were tea and cakes on the table.

'Sorry' started I.

'*Pas du problem*' Mrs Alford smiled at me. 'Sit down quickly.'

I obeyed.

'We hoped that you introduce your mystery brunette to us' winked she.

I suspected that my stepmother and stepfather discussed my private life, and I didn't want to make them sad. I thought to give them a few days to plan my fictive marriage.

'What kind of brunette?' I asked innocently.

'That brunette who made you miss the beginning of the second act' explicated Mrs Alford.

'Ah, that one! She's just a...' What could I have said? Stella's role changed too fast. My impression on Friday night was in contrast to my opinion on Monday evening. 'She's a friend of mine'.

Thanks to the new topic, we started to argue about our reading. Also, they argued, and I listened to them.

At about 4:40 pm, I paid the bill, and after that, we took a short and slow walk towards Miss Evans' bookshop.

'I think...' Mrs Alford said. 'I'll buy more of Phillips novels.'

Mr Cartwright answered something, and I turned into the side street where the bookshop was. At the next moment, I saw Aryan Singh, who had just walked out the door of the store, look at me in alarm and start to run. I threw down my book and ran after him. I was faster than Singh, so I caught him and pushed him against the wall.

'She already was dead… Trust me. When Preeti and I entered the store, Miss Evans was dead.' He spoke in a pleading tone.

'Show me' ordered I.

We walked back to the store where Preeti Singh and Mrs Alford's company discussed.

'It seemed that was an accident', explained Mrs Singh, terrified. 'Believe me, Mr Morgan, Aryan was horrified by the sight of the body. You have to believe me.'

I had not to.

'Is there anyone else in the store?' asked I.

Preeti Singh shook her head.

'I think not.'

'Right. Wait here and call the police' I turned to Mrs Alford, who nodded.

I wanted to check the crime scene before my colleague arrived. What kind of accident killed Miss Evans? Strange thing. I never thought something like that could happen to her.

'She's in the back, fell off the ladder.' That was Preeti Singh's voice.

I walked across the bookshelves with great care. Miss Evans' body was lying on the floor next to the ladder. There was an open book near her head. I crouched down to observe the body. At first sight, it seemed she had tried to take a book off the top shelf, lost her balance, after then, she broke her neck. But why were there bruises on her neck, as if somebody strangled her?

'Who are you, Sir? What are you doing here? It's a crime scene.'

I didn't know that policeman, and he didn't know me. I stood up.

'Sean Morgan, ex-Chief Inspector, Constable.'

'An ex-Chief Inspector? Bravo. Please leave the store and wait outside' pointed towards the door.

'Yes, Constable.' I replied. However, I didn't think he saluted or offered coffee, but he very quickly removed me from the scene. Suspicious.

'What do you think, Sean?' whispered Mrs Alford excitedly.

'Later.' I could not say more because I saw an old *buddy*, the great Chief Inspector Wallace, who was the best friend of my loved Superintendent Charles Laverton. What can I say? Laverton and I... So, he never preferred my investigative method. I noticed a few minutes later, when the police officer was already in the bookshop: 'Quick investigation'.

Very quick indeed.

Wallace was in there for five minutes, interrogating Aryan and Preeti Singh, but not me. The great Chief Inspector said that I constantly was misinterpreting what I saw. An unreliable witness—that was me.

'I don't like that man. He didn't introduce himself and didn't ask me,' Mrs Alford murmured and quickly ate two sandwiches.

There was the Bianchis' coffee shop, our current headquarters.

'You're right' agreed Mr Cartwright. 'Miss Evans was an accurate person, used that ladder every day. I don't understand. If I remember well, on the top shelves, there were empty... Sean, you were in there. Did you see the top shelves?'

'They weren't empty. Various books lay in disarray...' I replied thoughtfully. Cartwright said it right; Miss Evans liked the order. Liked? It was her religion. The books lined her shelves as the soldiers on parade. That was the second fault, and I was hoping to find more.

The brainstorming started, and I was watching.

'I think the motivation is the jealousy' explained Mrs Alford. 'Motivation—is that the right word, Sean?'

'Motivation, yes.'

Mrs Alford smiled with a shining face of pride.

'Thank you. So there should be somewhere a secret lover' continued she.

She liked that secret lover theme so much, and she couldn't think of anything else.

'Maybe' noticed Mr Brown doubtfully. 'But I heard before that Miss Evans was a cryptographer in the 1980s. Those were turbulent times: the Cold War was nearing its end, the Berlin Wall was torn down, and the Soviet Union was on the verge of complete collapse. We felt that the whole world changed. I think Miss Evans knew something dangerous. That was why she was killed—perhaps—by Russians.'

Yes. Mr Brown bought the special edition *James Bond* collection last month and already watched it twice. My information is so accurate because I have watched *The World Is Not Enough*—for Sophie Marceau—with him... twice. Even then, that theory wasn't incredible. If Miss Evans had worked for the Government, she would have had many enemies. I must check that information.

'Terrible, sorry, both of you are wrong', Mr Cartwright said, sipping a café latte. 'This is a straightforward case, you know. Miss Evans had a bookshop, right? The motivation could only be a book... a scarce, expensive book... like a mediaeval codex or the Apocrypha. What do you think, Sean?'

'I think there are three excellent motivations, but we haven't any evidence' I responded, and already thought the next step: visiting the body.

Sometime later, our special brainstorming was over. I bought a dozen of sandwiches and took a tour of the morgue. Doctor Robertson—my conspirator—was there.

'You came at the right time, Morgan. I'm hungry like a wolf.' Robertson took the package out of my hand—Robertson was always hungry like a wolf. 'The granny, right?' he asked, but didn't look at me, just tore the paper.

'Right' nodded I. 'She was strangled, I think.'

'You think very well, Morgan' he said, and took a bite of the first sandwich. 'The old mummy...'

That was Professor Grant, the head of the morgue.

'The old mummy established the cause of the death was a strong pressure on the jugular vein.'

'By what?'

'By human hand, Morgan… but Chief Inspector Wallace claims that was an accident, and the granny's scarf got caught in the ladder. That scarf caused the bruises… We didn't find any scarf among the evidence, and the photographers are not even aware of it. The prof should verify Wallace's theory, but without a killing tool… There wasn't any scarf, right?'

'I didn't see it.'

Robertson grinned at me.

'Wallace is an idiot… Professor Grant said that.'

Who am I to argue with a professor?

■—■—■—■□■—■—■—■

No matter how Wallace customizes the autopsy report, that scarf didn't exist, and Miss Evans was murdered. I must know Miss Evans' character and life; I should talk to other members of that book club. I planned those interrogations the next day. Notably, there was a curious aspect: our murderer was inexperienced and clumsy. Wallace's scarf idea was better than his ladder accident. At that moment, I had two conclusions. First, he wasn't a professional assassin. Second, that may have been the first murder that he committed—and that fact gave me an advantage.

At dawn, I suddenly recognized that I hadn't thought about Stella for hours. I was too tired. Stella—I sighed, turned left and continued sleeping.

FIVE

MY BRAIN WORKS like an archive: what I hear or see is stored, and I can recall it when I need it. I had information about the club members, and that morning, they lined up. While running, I devised a strategy: a quick breakfast at the Bianchis, and the work could begin.

Lucy Taylor was the first on my list. She worked as a barista in a coffee bar. She had mentioned to Judith Lynch two weeks ago when Taylor had talked about a guy who had been reading the same book as her and came into the coffee bar. I didn't remember the whole story, but I assumed that it hadn't a happy ending. So Lucy Taylor had talked about her job and named the street. That was enough for me.

I found that place very easily entered and walked to the counter. I had to wait in line because there were two people in front of me. I looked around; that was a usual place decorated with colourful photos of young and happy people who drank coffee. It all pointed out that you will be young and happy if you drink coffee here. I waited patiently; then, it was my turn.

'Good morning, Miss Taylor!' I started very politely.

'Good... What are you doing here?' She wondered.

'As a matter of fact, I would like to ask Mocha if it's possible, and I would like to ask something about Miss Evans, Miss Taylor.'

'We haven't Mocha, Sir. Please choose from the list' she pointed to a laminated board on the counter. She was unkind and eyed me suspiciously.

'Right. Then... I want to ask... Caramel Cortado.'

'Caramel Cortado' she repeated and turned toward the coffee machine.

'Miss Taylor, if I know well, you have been a member of the book club for six months. Perhaps Miss Evans talked about somebody who didn't like her or whom she was afraid of.'

Lucy Taylor didn't answer me, just made my coffee conscientiously.

'£4.20.' she said finally

I paid, and after that, she put the cup on the counter.

'Nazi!' she cried and spilt the coffee on my chest. 'He's a Nazi cop!' And she introduced me in a way I couldn't have expected to be so good.

I like Caramel Cortado, but not on my coat. So I hurried home and changed clothes. It was sure if Lucy Taylor knew something, she never told me. I accepted that.

The second round was Judith Lynch and Marthe Laroche. They often chatted about their favourite supermarket, and if I was lucky, I could talk to both of them because they usually shop together.

And I was fortunate. I found Mrs Lynch and Mrs Laroche among the vegetables and fruits.

'Oh, poor Emily! She was so kind' noted Mrs Lynch. 'That ladder was too dangerous. I told her many times.'

'At her age' added Mrs Laroche. 'Sad story.'

'Do you know what will happen to her bookshop? They closed, or she had any relatives who took over the business?'

'No… she never told about any relatives. I think she hadn't family; she was alone,' explained Mrs Laroche while examining the sprouts. 'She received a very nice postcard at last Christmas. She put it on the wall behind the cash register. When I asked her, she told me that an old friend had written it… Oh! We have to inform that man, haven't we?'

'I think so' responded I. 'Do you remember his name?'

'Harvey… With love, Harley—he wrote.'

Harvey—it was not too much, just a first name, and I should be glad it wasn't John or Will. By the way, he was not Doctor Hughes because his first name was George.

After shopping, I invited them for a coffee. That place was cosy, the cakes were sugar-free, and my second Caramel Cortado was tasty. We talked for two hours, but I finally had that name, nothing else.

■—■—■—■□■—■—■—■

The Singhs lived in an Edwardian house. I knew their address because they had once ordered some books from Miss Evans, who had delivered them personally. Miss Evans noted the address on paper, which was lying on the counter. I saw it by accident and thought it was a costly area.

I hoped they were home. I rang, carrying a bottle of wine—my mother said: *a guest always brings a gift, especially an uninvited one.* Preeti Singh opened the door; she looked surprised but still invited me. She wore a lilac saree—that was strange; she usually wore modern clothes, not traditional ones in the club.

'Aryan's working' started she.

'On a new book?'

'A new book?'

'Margaret White, I think.'

'How do you know?... Sorry, it was a stupid question. You're a cop, of course, you know, right?' She was confused and wrinkled her saree. 'You know, Aryan did nothing wrong.'

'He did anything, right? What was that?'

She already seemed alarmed.

'Mrs Singh, what did he do?'

'I searched Miss Evans' notebook', answered Aryan Singh, who wasn't working yet.

'What kind of notebook?'

'I think it would be better that I'll tell you everything, Mr Morgan.'

'It would be better' nodded Preeti Singh. 'I make a tea.'

A few minutes later, I sat in a Scandinavian-styled, very comfortable armchair and waited curiously for for Aryan

Singh's confession, while his wife served us tea. Preeti Singh finally took a seat next to her husband. There was a little pause, and after that, Aryan Singh started to speak.

'As you know, I wrote romance novels as Margaret White. My readers love them, and that business pays quite well, but for a few months, I haven't had any idea. I just sat at my laptop watching the empty page, but my publishing house wants the next one in a few weeks. Do you understand?'

I tried to be understanding.

'That's why you went to the book club, I guess.'

'Yes, exactly, Mr Morgan. I hoped it would inspire me.'

'It was quite striking to write everything' noted I. 'Never mind. Continue.'

Aryan Singh drank a sip of tea.

'Emily… Miss Evans wrote novels, too. Her pseudonym was Stanley Phillips…'

That surprised me.

'Wait a moment' interrupted I. 'It wasn't fair that Miss Evans proposed her novel, was it?'

'That was Judith who proposed a Stanley Phillips novel, not Emily.'

'I see.' I waved to him to speak.

'Right…' he swallowed. 'Emily had a small rose pattern notebook. She wrote everything in it. Characters' name, plot outline and all kinds of details, you know?'

I nodded.

'She often left the notebook on her desk…'

'Where is her desk? I cannot remember.'

'It's in the back room, her storage room.'

'And?'

'And when I saw Emily's body on the floor, I thought she wouldn't be able to use it anymore, but I would. How many ideas were in it?'

'And you find it?'

'No. I think she closed it in a drawer… I thoroughly searched the desk and around the cash register, but found nothing. After that, I was scared to death of what I had done, and you came… What do you want to do, Mr Morgan?' He looked at me with a contrite face.

'I'm an ex-cop, and let's pretend I didn't hear anything. Right? In return, you answer my questions. It's a good deal for you' said I.

Aryan Singh immediately agreed, and his wife sighed with relief: 'Thank you!'

I didn't mention if anybody else—not Wallace—led that investigation, they could have been in big trouble. They were already frightened enough.

■—■—■—■□■—■—■—■

I created my special investigation board using copy paper, after I wrote the names of the club members. My board was so modest yet. Next to Aryan and Preeti Singh, I noticed Margaret White and rose pattern notebook. Emily Evans had founded a mall company: Doctor Hughes, Harvey and Stanley Philipps. I knew the time of the death: between 4:30 and 4:45—as Aryan Singh confirmed—, the place: in the bookshop, and the method: she was strangled by a strong and determined person—instead a man than a woman. So I had *means* and *opportunity*, but I didn't have any *motivation.*

After some thought, I cancelled the members' names from the murderer list—my instincts told me to look elsewhere. As a result, I had two directions. First, the earlier life—I must talk with Doctor Hughes and find that secretly Harvey. Second, there is somebody or something in her current life, I mean, from the last few years. I tried to call Doctor Hughes several times, but there was no answer; after that, I left a very touching message, hoping he would call me back. Finding Harvey was harder. I heard about a Christmas card—that's all.

I studied many websites, such as *Famous Oxonians, Old Students of Oxford University*, and similar. I read about Emily Evans a lot, but I didn't find any mention of Harvey. If it was a nickname, I didn't get much use out of it.

I downloaded some photos and was trying to enlarge them and identify Miss Evans when somebody rang. Queer. I waited for nobody. I folded my board and hid it with my act.

There was Mr Brown and Mr Cartwright.

'Good evening, Sean! I bet you barely ate anything today' entered Mr Brown. 'We made for you a shepherd's pie, fruit salad and lemon biscuits. I'm sure you are working all day… Don't worry. You don't need to talk about the investigation. I understand.'

'You read me like an open book' I answered.

Mr Brown was right. My last meal was a slice of sugar-free cheesecake at about 11:30 am, and then it was about

8 pm. When he mentioned the shepherd's pie, I got hungry. I led them into my living room and offered a drink.

'No, thank you. We don't want to bother you, but we investigated too… just a little bit' noticed Mr Cartwright smiling.

'Really?'

'Oh, yes. And we collected articles' he handed me a thick folder. I didn't even notice it, perhaps because of the pie. 'I hope it will be beneficial.'

I hope so.

■—■—■—■☐■—■—■—■

The shepherd's pie was excellent and gave a new impetus to my work. I began to select Mr Cartwright's articles, which were indeed interesting, amusing, and valuable. I found a remarkable one, which was about Miss Evans' career in the Bodleian Library. Evans had worked there for ten years after the bookshop opened. She had a special Oxonian section in there for the students and applied for the student discount. She said: *I want to help the children. Ipsa scientia potestat est—knowledge is power. I mean, everyone has the right to learn, to make dreams come true.* She was a genuine philanthropist; she had tortured me to death, just me. Perhaps she didn't like the police officers, thinking all of them were mindless toy soldiers. As fate would have it, one of them tried to catch her killer.

I fell asleep. I didn't know when or how, but I fell asleep, covering my papers. Phone ringing awoke me—unknown number. I didn't want to talk to anyone, but finally, I picked up the phone.

'Morgan' said I, yawning.

'It's Stella. May I come in?'

I thought I was dreaming.

'Beg your pardon?'

'Sean, please let me in.' She hung up the phone.

At the next second, somebody rang.

I collected and hid the papers, and after that, I went to the door.

A few minutes later, she was in the middle of my dining room. She said as much as was necessary: nothing, just took off her coat.

SIX

YES, I KNOW I'm an idiot. I played such a game in which I could lose. Stella never divorced her well-paid husband and never gave up her brilliant social life for a country house. I need to see clearly: I was just a reserve player for her, not more. Why did I accept this situation? I could not imagine. That could be better than nothing.

Stella left around 6 am. We didn't promise anything to each other, and I didn't wait for anything to happen. If she came, then came; if she didn't, what could I do?

Not long after, I started my usual running. At the second intersection, I saw an old lady who could barely walk. She wanted to cross the zebra crossing and looked around very anxiously. I had much time, I thought, to help her.

'May I, Mme?' I approached her.

She turned to me, nodded and smiled.

I stepped next to me, and after that, she took a little bottle out of her handbag and sprayed some pungent, smelly gas on my face. She was so quick, no hesitating. I started to cry, my vision became blurry more and more suddenly, everything went black, and I finally went blind. That happened in a matter of seconds. I heard a car heading towards me slow down and stop. Its door opened, and they pushed me in—I felt like there were more people. Finally, the car engine roared.

'Terrible sorry, Mr Morgan. Unfortunately, I had to take precautions. Don't worry, your temporary blindness will go away within a few hours' explained a male voice. He spoke calmly, in a polite tone, as if we had met at a cheerful garden party. 'It is necessary for me to maintain my anonymity. My name cannot be mentioned in connection with Emily's death. You need to understand it, right?'

I understood, so I nodded.

'Good. In fact, I consulted with Chief Inspector Wallace, but I wasn't delighted with what he said. I think he rushed things. That scarf theory is very...'

'Stupid' I finished the sentence.

'Yes, stupid. So, as I know, you were at the crime scene before the police arrived. You did talk with Doctor Robertson and the club members, too. I assume you have a better idea.'

'I'm afraid not, Sir. I have to explore Miss Evans' past. First, her bookshop, her home, and her will.'

'It isn't necessary, believe me. We examined those places very thoroughly and didn't find any trace. About her will... So, she left all her wealth at the Bodleian Library. I don't think anyone would have been killed for that.'

I think so.

'What about the rose pattern notebook?' I asked.

'You know the notebook, don't you? Good. Our men already have checked it.'

'It isn't necessary, Sir—as you would say. Miss Evans used that for writing novels. Every data is just a fiction.'

'Ohm… Thank you, Mr Morgan. However, I'm sure our men have already figured this out.'

'Not at all, Harvey,' I noticed to test my hypothesis.

'Clever boy. The postcard, right?'

'Yes, Sir.'

'I would like to keep this information between us, Mr Morgan, and to prove my good intentions, I'll say one more thing. A long time ago, Emily and I… so we were close friends in Oxford and after, that's why I want to know every circulation of her death.'

He didn't say any news.

'I see, Sir, and if I suppose well, Miss Evans' death has no connection to our shared past.'

'Correct. Now, please answer me. What do you think about Emily's death?'

Dear Harvey, both of us know exactly what I think; otherwise, we wouldn't be here. So why is this excessive politeness necessary? Madness. It's like an episode from *The Crown*. Right. I could use that tone and discuss the flowers of Buckingham Palace.

'I think…' I started and took my time a little bit. 'I think somebody strangled Miss Evans after then arranged the scene for the performance.'

'But who?'

'I hoped you told me, Sir.'

There was a pause. Harvey could have pushed me out of the moving car and left me in the middle of the road blindly and helplessly. Fortunately, Harvey was a real gentleman.

'Interesting situation' noticed he. 'If the key is not the past...'

'May the present be?'

'In that case, it's your business. You can move unnoticed, not me. What will be your next step?'

I wish I knew.

'I'll see if I can see, Sir.'

'Nice to talk to you, Mr Morgan... At the next corner, you get out of the car. If you have something to say, post an ad in *The Times*. Choose the category *Birthday*, write something and use Emily's name. Do you understand it?'

'I do.'

'Good. Be careful, Mr Morgan.'

The car stopped, and they dragged me out into the street. Because I was dealing with an Oxford graduate personality, I tried to express myself in a sophisticated manner as Sir Percy Blackney: *sink me.*

I didn't know whether I should feel panicked or not. I trusted Harvey like I trusted a Somali pirate. There was fifty per cent that he told the truth, but there were more than fifty.

Finally, I decided to wait for the result in my apartment. It was easier than I thought because they brought me to the house where I lived. It was a very bizarre survival show on TV, but not too amusing. Somehow, I stumbled up the stairs to the front door, managed to open it, and was already inside. I accidentally knocked down a bowl or vase—it made a sharp sound when it broke—and hit the wall several times, making a mess in the bathroom while washing my face with cold water. Then I lay down on the bed. A few minutes later, I started to get bored, so I wanted to find my phone. Usually, I didn't take it with me for running, and I remembered leaving it on the console table in the living room. That was my new expedition.

After some clumsiness, I found the console table, not my phone—it was nowhere. That coincided with the realization that someone else was in the room. I based that statement on the strong menthol smell of e-cigarettes. I didn't smoke for five years and hated the menthol.

'Who are you?' I asked—not an exciting question.

That person didn't give any answer but pushed me against the wall.

'Not his face' said a hoarse voice.

So there were two guests in my living room.

I received a few punches in my stomach. It was hard to box blindly; I fell to the floor and got a few kicks, too. Finally, the hitman leaned over me.

'Get Stella out of your head, or I get with a hammer, right?' He kicked me in the kidney as confirmation.

That surprised me. Not the kicking, but rather the mention of Stella's name. Honestly, I assumed the hitmen worked for Harvey; instead, Stella's husband entered my life. My apartment was starting to get crowded.

■—■—■—■☐■—■—■—■

I lingered on the floor for a few minutes, and after that, my vision slowly returned. First, I could see great light spots, after the outlines of objects, and at last, after some transition, the order was restored.

I had two problems: Stella and Miss Evans's death. I ignored Stella and focused on Miss Evans—a dead person who deserves more attention. I've thought about it several times, but I always come to the same conclusion: her personality was the origin.

I tidied up my apartment and swept up the pieces of the broken vase. Meanwhile, I found Stanley Phillips' book—my last required reading. Its title was so melodramatic: *Frozen Roses*. A strange thought flashed through my mind: if Miss Evans had been a cryptographer, she had hidden details in her novels. That's it! First, I bought a dozen sandwiches in Bianchi's coffee shop, after which I hurried to the largest bookshop in the city.

'Could you please show me where I can find Stanley Phillips' novels?'

The bookseller, a young woman with glasses, looked at me strangely.

'My mother read the *Frozen Roses* and wanted the other ones too' explained I.

Then the young woman smiled at me very friendly. My explication dispelled her suspicions.

'That way, please' she waved, and I followed her.

The old *boy* Stanley wrote eight thick volumes, so I needed a shopper bag, decorated with with the name of the shop, and three slim, elegant, dark blue notebooks. I let them talk me into buying the keychain, pens and metal fridge magnet, and I gave half a dozen bookmarks as a gift.

My new strategy was reading Miss Evans' complete works. I hoped to find some information or trace among the many romances. I started *Frozen Roses*, but I was reading chapter one when my phone began to ring. That was Doctor Hughes, who invited me to his consulting room at 4 pm—I had totally forgotten my latest dramatic call. He said I was deeply traumatized 'cause of Miss Evans' death and needed to talk to him. I wanted to meet him, so I replied with a polite "yes."

After that, I continued to read… more precisely, I wanted to continue, but my phone rang again. Another invitation. At that time, Mr Brown and Mr Cartwright asked for dinner: roast lamb with potatoes—a new recipe. I explained to them that I worked hard. It seemed they understood, and they promised to bring me a portion of it. I said many thanks.

I waited for a few minutes. Perhaps Mrs Alford called me. I made coffee, but it was nothing. So, I read the book.

■—■—■—■□■—■—■—■

I arrived at Doctor Hughes' waiting room at 3:55 pm. There were Rorschach tests on the wall. I liked to look at them, but they reminded me of the *black spot* in *Treasure Island*—Doctor Hughes said that completely reflected my personality. I didn't have much time to look around at that time because his assistant—an older woman—smiled at me and led me in.

'Sean, I'm so glad to come. I received your message… You cannot imagine how much I waited for you. Please, take a seat' he greeted with unusual enthusiasm.

'Thank you' I said and sank into the armchair.

'Terrible thing, isn't it?' he said after then sat down. 'Dear Emily! What a tragedy! Honestly, I don't understand how it happened. It's all so pointless…' He just talked and talked without end.

I slowly began to realize that was reverse therapy. Doctor Hughes spoke, and I listened to him, nodding occasionally or responding with a simple "yes." However, that was not a mere waste of time. Hughes mentioned a man—Miss Alford probably would name a secret lover. Miss Evans had met that mystery man a few years ago at the London Book Fair. Miss Evans and that man had been dating for months, but suddenly, he had disappeared, and she hadn't spoken to him anymore. Unfortunately, Hughes had never met him, but still described him as an elegant, very polite person. I felt that the mysterious, sleek man was important; I had to find him.

Finally, Doctor Hughes thanked me for the conservation and made an appointment for the following Friday. I allowed it—who knows?

■—■—■—■□■—■—■—■

I don't know much about writing novels, but I remember well Mrs Belfrag, my literature teacher in the school. She had always said that the authors use some elements of reality in their works. Miss Evans probably displayed that male character in one of her romance stories. It would be better if Doctor Hughes knew the exact year.

I went home and then made a timeline of Miss Evans' novels. She had written the first one in 2014 and the last one, *Frozen Roses*, in January 2025. It was Friday evening, and I decided to spend my weekend reading, taking notes, and analysing. But first, I posted an ad in *The Times*. That was so simple: *Mr and Mrs Phillips, congratulations on the twin! I hope you are all well. With love, Emily Evans...* I expected a quick answer.

SEVEN

I SLEPT JUST for a few hours, but I was chasing a phantom, and I didn't know which information would be necessary. I created Excel tables and lists of characters' names—with special attention to male ones—times, places, and summaries, and a collection of stories filling almost two of my exclusive notebooks. I had a timeline of the publication, as I mentioned before, and another of the plots of the novels. I thought I had noticed everything, yet in the end, I felt that I was getting further and further away from the goal.

That was Sunday evening. I rightly hoped that if I slept well, new thoughts would come the next day. So, I peacefully laid my head on the pillow and fell asleep immediately.

That Monday started as usual. I ran my turn, took a shower, and then went to Mr and Mrs Bianchi's coffee shop. I ate three toothsome sandwiches and drank a strong coffee—I didn't know what kind of it was Mr Bianchi chose for me. Homeward, I took a long walk.

Harvey didn't call me yet. I slowly began to accept that I would have to get by without him.

I was sitting at my desk studying my *lovely* tables when somebody rang. I was sure that it was Mr Brown who brought some cakes, and maybe some data. I was wrong. Wallace stood on my doorstep.

'Chief Superintendent Dugdale wants to see you, Morgan. Get a suit. Now!'—Nothing good morning or something else.

I nodded. I don't argue with a Chief Superintendent. Moreover, Dugdale was Laverton's ex-father-in-law— Laverton's first wife died three years ago. That didn't mean anything good. Did Wallace notice my private investigation? Maybe one of the club members could tell him about it. Or Harvey…? Who knows?

Finally, I followed Wallace, wearing my dark grey suit with a white shirt and a very boring greyish blue tie—also my unofficial police uniform.

■—■—■—■□■—■—■—■

Dugdale's office was on the third level, at the end of the corridor. You have to go through the corridor to get there. Two guys stood in front of one of the glass doors, grinning. I didn't understand what they found so funny until I walked past them. The bigger one smelled of menthol cigarettes. It was worth the trip; I finally got to see them *en face*.

In Dugdale's office, there was the Chief Superintendent himself and my loved buddy, Laverton. Wallace came with me and closed the door. Three against one, I didn't have much of a chance.

'You arrived just in time, Morgan' Dugdale started because he had the highest rank. He was sitting at his impressive desk. 'I don't have time anyway, especially for cockfights... So, if I know well, there is a personal opposite between Superintendent Laverton and you. I hate this thing. The police must be unified. I cannot stand the internal strife, and it's very destructive.'

Laverton, who stood next to Dugdale, nodded enthusiastically, and so did Wallace. I couldn't imagine what I was doing there.

'The Superintendent informed me you despised him so much that you seduced his wife...'

What?

A moment and everything came together. Two police-hitmen on the corridor, Laverton and his ex-father-in-law. Damned! Stella was Laverton's second wife.

'You mean, Chief Superintendent, Stella Laverton was she, right?' I said as proof of my hypothesis.

'How dare you say her name?' Laverton cried dramatically as a Shakespearian actor.

'Gentlemen, calm down' waved Dugdale. 'We need to solve this problem in a civilized way.'

In a civilized way with hitmen? That was a very unique line of thought.

'Apologize for my behaviour, Sir.' Laverton excused himself as a good boy.

'Not at all, Charles' answered the permissive ex-father-in-law. 'So, our problem is… Let's say so. Mr Morgan has too much free time. I think we were too hasty when we retired you, Chief Inspector. That's why we decided to change our decision regarding your retirement.' He took a short break, and I was sure I wouldn't be grateful even though it sounded good. 'You must take up your new position in Lower Oak within thirty days.'

Lower Oak, I've never heard about that place. I suspected it was in the middle of nowhere.

'Do you have any question, Morgan?'

I had many questions, but he wouldn't answer anyway.

'Right. You'll receive the official command in writing in a few days. Do you understand it, Morgan?'

'I understand well, Chief Superintendent.'

'Dismissed.'

'Thank you, Sir.'

On my way out, I made sure to close the door softly. After that, I had to leave in front of my two buddies.

'I heard that Lower Oak is a perilous place,' said one of them.

'Yes' admitted the other one. 'There's a lot of bike theft around here… and stray sheep and cows' he started to laugh.

I'm glad you're having a good time. Clowns!

■—■—■—■□■—■—■—■

My situation was... extraordinary. I needed time to think about it. Lower Oak is due in thirty days, so it's been moved to the unimportant section. By the way, I wanted to live in country a few days ago. I got it.

What about Stella? My relationship with Stella was over clearly and definitely. But what about Miss Evans? Yes. As if we had drifted apart... and then the phone call came.

'Morgan.'

'I'm glad to hear you, Sir. You posted an ad in *The Times* last Sunday' said a pleasant female voice.

Great timing.

'What can I do for you, Sir? asked she.

'I need some information about Miss Evans.'

'Yes, Sir.'

'Did Miss Evans participate in the London Book Fair every year?'

'Wait a moment, Sir, I check it...' I heard typing. 'Miss Evans participated in the London Book Fair for the first time in 2001 until 2018. She had already not participated in 2019 and had not registered. 2018 was the last year, Sir.'

2018, I noticed it. If that book fair was the fatal one, the mysterious lover could have appeared even then.

'Thank you. Could you please send me the list of participants?'

'Which years, Sir?'

'From 2015 until 2018 if it is possible.' Our guy only probably came out in 2018. A year-by-year comparison might be helpful.

'No problem, Sir. I'll send it by e-mail as soon as possible. Anything else?'

'At this moment, I'm afraid nothing. Thank you.'

'I see, Sir. Next time, you don't need to post an ad; please call me at this number. Have a nice day, Sir!' She hung up the phone.

Sometimes, things happen so easily.

▪—▪—▪—▪▢▪—▪—▪—▪

I recall that Miss Evans published a novel around 2018, and I thought I had found the solution there. I hurried home and checked my tables at once. I got it: *Man with Secrets* (2019). How stupid was I! I should have guessed from the title—by the way, I have to confess I used to think the main character was Harvey.

Man with Secrets—his name was Paul Rifkin. At first, he was kind, polite, and intelligent, like a dream, but later it turned out that the man was selfish and cruel. I would say he was a typical narcissistic psychopath. Don't worry! There is no physical abuse, just psychological. There were some broken-hearted women in the story, and one of them could confront him—I think that was Miss Evans herself. Rifkin—the big bad wolf—finally went to prison for tax fraud—what a happy end!

So, Miss Evans met our guy at the 2018 London Book Fair. As Doctor Hughes said, the happiness had lasted a few months. Miss Evans had been left alone and written a novel about her sad romance, which was published in 2019.

Strange. If our man had wanted revenge for the book, why was he waiting for six years? I assumed he worked for a publishing house, or, if not, that he was keeping an eye on the market and the new books. That was the weakness of my theory, but it was the only one I had at that moment.

So, I needed the list of participants, and trusting in Miss Evans' cryptographic expertise I could identify that mystery Paul Rifkin.

■—■—■—■□■—■—■—■

I didn't change my clothes—and I did well. I had a phone call from Timothy Ross & Sons Solicitors. I was asked to visit them at 3 pm. They didn't say why, just that it was urgent. I read about them online: Timothy and his sons dealt with family matters. My first thought was Stella, but if she filed a complaint against me—for example, sexual adults –they wouldn't have sent me to the rainiest part of England but made me arrested. In any case, I don't think that Laverton wants to take his wife's infidelities to court. I didn't have any other tips.

At 2:50 pm, I entered Ross' office. A young, friendly assistant in a tight suit and stilettos greeted me and asked me to wait for a few minutes because I arrived earlier. Apropos, she didn't ask my name or what I was doing there. She knew everything about me, but I knew nothing.

She opened the solicitor's door at precisely 3 pm.

Mr Ross was an old-fashioned, well-dressed, and high-priced lawyer.

'Please come in, Mr Morgan. Take a seat' he shook my hand—that was firm handshake.

A few seconds later, he sat in his comfortable black leather armchair and began to leaf through the papers lying in front of him on the desk. Then, he suddenly looked up.

'Miss Emily Evans was my client, you know.'

That surprised me quite a bit.

'One of the best' continued he. 'A month ago she visited me, gave me a closed package and an envelope with only strange condition. I'll have to open the envelope if I'm informed of her death. I confess, then I found it ridiculous. I couldn't imagine it would be happened... You know I spent the last week in Scotland; I just saw her obituary this morning in *The Oxford Times*. What a tragedy!...' His sorrow seemed sincere. 'As she asked I opened the letter. I would like to read the part about you, Mr Morgan...'

I nodded.

'*In case of my death, dear Timothy, give the package to Chief Inspector Sean Morgan...* She wrote your address and phone number' explained dear Timothy. '*Say him England expects that every man will do his duty.* It's Admiral Horatio Nelson... So... this is typical of Emily.'

I didn't care if Ross thought I was an uneducated barbarian. However, I could quote Nelson's last letter to Lady Hamilton—obviously, Lady Hamilton was the reason for my interest.

'Miss Evans was a cryptographer, right?'

'I don't know, Mr Morgan... it is possible. A few months ago, I forgot the code of my safe—she was there sitting in that armchair…' He pointed that one in which I sat. 'She opened it in ten minutes… She found out in ten minutes. She was a genius… But now I give you this package, Mr Morgan.'

Dear Timothy talked for ten minutes—he was so curious about what was in my package. Since I suspected it might contain some evidence, I wanted to open it alone and home.

I cut the package's paper with a sharp knife and very carefully, but I found only a book: *Man with Secrets*. I was a little disappointed because I had waited for a letter written with a secret code or special equipment, such as a small chessboard with holes—as seen in spy movies. I examined both the wrapping paper and the book, compared to my copy, but found nothing. However, I would have been proud as I figured that novel was the key—with Harvey's help. After that, I remembered Miss Evans' words: "*…you cannot leave your earlier life, your profession, and you're unable to see the story from a different perspective*". Perhaps that's why she sent me the book. She had believed I found the real Paul Rifkin… Wait a moment! That also meant she had suspected something happened. The high-priced Ross mentioned Miss Evans' visit… A month ago… perhaps our guy and she had met about, Miss Evans had told something, and her mystery and cruel lover had panicked. What had happened then? What did Miss Evans know about that man? Love, romance novels, books—at first, they don't seem dangerous.

England expects that every man will do his duty—that was Miss Evans' message from beyond the grave. I understood well… I bet she had loved the crosswords and riddles, and she was a cryptographer… it followed that the book was a puzzle… she had hidden everything in it, and with her help, I was going to find Rifkin.

It would be easier if the lists had arrived yet, but at that moment, I had to get by without them.

I spread all of my notes on the bed. What did I know? I was sure the *Man with Secrets* was my Enigma, Paul Rifkin's real personality was the murderer, and Rifkin led me to him. What did I know about Rifkin? He was an attractive-looking personality, around fifty years old, elegant and polite. He lived in London, worked at a publishing house… In other words, he worked at a real publishing house, which required real detective work. I searched the list of all of the publishers in London. I started to check them in alphabetic order: time-consuming but effective.

Meanwhile, I had a brief conversation with Miss Alford—I didn't discuss my new position; I wanted to share it with her later, in person. She inquired about my private investigation and invited me to dinner the following evening. Half an hour later, Mr Brown and Mr Cartwright arrived with a massive box of sausage rolls. I didn't say any word about change—I didn't have time for that. Mr Cartwright brought some articles and told us that he and Mr Brown walked towards Miss Evans' bookshop that afternoon; it was closed, lifeless, and dark, with withered flowers and candles at the entrance, a sad sight.

I didn't want to seem impolite, so I made a tea, and we tested Mr Brown's tasty sausage rolls.

I was halfway through my ever-expanding list when Heather O'Neil rang. She was in a disturbed state of mind.

Constable Heather O'Neil was complicit in the last illegal activity. A few years ago, I had suggested she had passed the Sergeants' Exam. Unfortunately, Laverton had vetoed that. She was an intelligent, brave young woman. I thought she could have a great career.

'Is that true?' she asked, hurrying straight to my living room.

'Terrible sorry…' I could imagine what she might think of me.

'I guessed… Laverton had been in a perfect mood for days.' She sat down in the armchair by the window. 'I thought everything. If you are the superior offices in Lower Oak, you will accept my transfer request, Mr Mo…, sorry, Sir' she corrected herself with a smile.

'That's right… Heather, you really want that, don't you? I mean Mrs Laverton… you know…' It was a sensitive topic, but it would be better to talk about it.

'Mrs Laverton? What about Mrs Laverton?'

'Our loved Superintendent didn't inform you?

'I don't understand, Sir. Laverton said that you interfered with Wallace's investigation, and Chief Superintendent Dugdale changed your status,' explained. 'But now I'm curious about what's going with Mrs Laverton.'

I hesitated a few seconds.

'I'll tell you in Lower Oak.'

'Right. It's not important, I think.'

On the contrary.

'When you started the work in Lower Oak, Sir?'

'In thirty days.'

'So little time, Sir. You have *so much to do and so little time*... So you interfered in Wallace's investigation or not?' she demanded suspiciously.

Because of Harvey, I had to lie:

'I'm afraid this time not.'

'Why did I wait in front of your door for minutes?... Right, you'll tell it also in Lower Oak.'

I nodded.

'Then... I won't bother you, Chief Inspector Morgan. Have a nice idleness!' She winked at me, stood up, and hurried away.

▪—▪—▪—▪ ▢ ▪—▪—▪—▪

Around midnight, I was so tired. Just one more—I thought. All right. I decided the See Blue Publishing House was the last. It had been founded in 2017. Interesting. The managing director was Alfred R. Kinleyside, who had represented his company at the London Book Fair every year since 2018. According to the date, there was a chance he was our guy. Alfred R. Kinleyside... How did he become Paul Rifkin? Alfred R. Kinleyside—Paul Rifkin... If I highlighted the letters a and l from his forename, that was Al, like Alfred. R is the first letter of Rifkin. Kinleyside, I had three letters in his family name. Would that be the solution? Or did I complicate it? I didn't know.

I typed his name into the search box, and I found a sponsored article. What a coincidence! The next day, an unknown author signs his books in Foyles Bookshop. The publisher's head also attended the prestigious event because they were best friends. There was a big picture of the Kinleyside and that friend. He was a chubby guy, not the type to be a Don Juan. That wasn't how I imagined him. Perhaps he was different in real life than he appeared online.

I yawned a lot. Before I went to sleep, I bought a return ticket to London. The book signing starts at 3 pm. I will be home by evening, Mrs Alford's dinner party.

EIGHT

AS THE SONG said, it was *a foggy day in London town*, but I didn't feel sorrow or apathy. It was so exciting. I arrived at Foyles early, hoping to catch Kidneyside. When I entered, I stopped for a moment. A nice young woman approached me.

'Welcome to Foyles, Sir! Can I help you?'

'Thank you, and I think yes. You know, I search…'

'The book signing' nodded she. 'On the first level, Sir.'

'Thank you' repeated I. 'This book…' Yes, I brought my trap novel, *Man with Secrets*.

'Yes, I see. You can take it.'

We were polite to each other for a few sentences, and then I headed for the stairs. I was lucky. Kidneyside was standing next to the column and talking on the phone. I watched him, and then he noticed me; I smiled at him with a silly grin—as I imagined the book fans. He smiled back, waved, and a few seconds later finished the call.

'Nice to meet you!' I shook his hand at once. 'You're a great man!'

He was surprised but smiled unwaveringly.

'May I ask a sign, Sir?' Without waiting for an answer, I pushed the book cover under his nose.

The change was visible. At first, he was scared, then he started looking at me suspiciously.

'Are you Stanley Philipps, right?' I asked with a naive look.

'Who the hell told you that?' His voice was angry.

'That nice young lady at the entrance.'

'Stupid girl!' murmured he. 'You're wrong.' He turned his back and disappeared.

There was no tangible evidence, but what I saw on his face proved it for me.

Finally, I chose four romance novels and bought them—as if I were a regular customer.

On the train, I thought about Kinleyside. I had to check his alibi—I had some friends from Scotland Yard—and explore his motivation. I had to be very cautious because there was ten per cent of his innocence. If his character was in Miss Evans' novel, I thought the motivation had to be there. Paul Rifkin was arrested and charged with tax fraud. Tax fraud… what did that mean?

When I arrived home, the mail from Harvey was waiting for me. Nice lists, but I had an invitation, so I put on an elegant suit and carried the new books, then closed my door. Goodbye, Kinleyside! See you later!

■—■—■—■□■—■—■—■

'You're so cruel!' Mrs Alford sighed.

We were sitting at her mahogany dining table. There was the whole family's treasure, from Georgian candlesticks, cutlery, and Empire porcelains to Baroque wine glasses. Mrs Alford asked me about Miss Evans' death, but I didn't say a word.

'No' I protested. I wasn't cruel; I was only careful.

'Sophia, my darling, you have to understand. Sean is an ex-police officer' Gérard tried to help me.

At that moment, I found out that my special situation was an excellent *camouflage*.

'As a matter of fact…' started I, after then I talked about Stella and my new position.

Mrs Alford cried, because she imagined more romantic story than I had. And while she wiped her tears, she comforted me.

'Where is Lower Oak?' asked Gérard.

'In Norfolk, South of Norwich.'

'Which road leads there? We'll visit you, Sean' sniffed Mrs Alford. 'It's a scandal! They had to promote you, not send to the end of the word.'

'Norfolk isn't the end of the world, my dear' he reassured her.

'The end of the civilized world' stated Mrs Alford.

'I think we will celebrate. Sean got his job back. I think this would be a promising start' suggested Gérard. 'Champagne!'

Mrs Alford loved the champagne and didn't say no.

Two hours and a few bottles of champagne later, I entered my apartment. Champagne went straight to my head.

It may be better to leave work until tomorrow. I spread out on the bed like a countess fan after an old-fashioned ball. I felt dizzy, but I had an extraordinary feeling. The book *Man with Secrets*, I left it on my bedside table, but at that moment, it wasn't there… I must be remembering wrong. I closed my eyes…

NINE

WHILE RUNNING, I thought about Gérard's words: promising start. That morning, I felt that was a promising start indeed; I caught Mr. Alfred R. Kinleyside—a quick shower, after then breakfast at the Bianchis.

Then the big surprise came. My notes, files, tables, the whole board, and the books—Stanley Philipps' complete works, both of *Man with Secrets*—all disappeared. They cleaned my secret drawer, my laptop and my bedside table They took my empty notebook too. I suspected Harvey ordered the general cleaning after I went to Mrs Alford. Was I angry? Yes! I did not finish that investigation, did had no evidence, and did did not know Kinleyside's motivation—that latter annoyed me the most. I immediately called the secret connection: *This phone number cannot be associated with any account* was the response.

I should have been satisfied because it meant I had Miss Evans' murderer, but I had many unanswered questions. Right, Harvey had the right of priority at the same time; the work was nevertheless shared. I had rights, too. I wanted to know why Kinleyside had killed Miss Evans and what had happened a month ago.

■—■—■—■□■—■—■—■

Miss Evans' problem was approximately solved, and I could concentrate on my issues like packing and official business, but first, I must talk with Mr Brown. Last evening, I asked Mrs Alford not to tell anyone about my new position. She always was an understanding woman. There was nothing left to do but call Mr Brown. We agreed to meet at his favourite French restaurant at 1 pm.

'Lower Oak? I know that town. Very nice place' noticed Mr Cartwright. 'Only temporary, I think.'

'I think so' added Mr Brown enthusiastically.

I didn't want to ruin their good mood, so I nodded.

'In thirty days? Many tasks await you. We help you, of course; you can count on us, Sean.'

'You're very kind, John, both of you.'

'We will miss you, Sean… But what is modern technology for? If you'll need a good company or a new recipe, call us. Don't be shy!'

'I'll call you, I swear' I responded with a smile, because I could see myself in that God-forsaken police station, and I'd have only one problem: what kind of cake I bake. I'll open a little patisserie to spend time.

'And… what about your… hobby, Sean?'

I knew well Mr Cartwright through my private investigation.

'Dead end. I hoped that I found the solution to Miss Evans' novels, but my ship ran aground.' That was half true.

'I'm sorry to hear that... you know we were thinking the same thing as you.' Mr Cartwright leaned closer. '*Man with Secrets*—I'm sure that was the key... Honestly, first I guessed *Frozen Roses*...'

'We argued about this for hours' Mr Brown told. 'It was funny... John said that *Paul Rifkin* from *Man with Secrets* was the same person as *Alfred Seaborn* from *Frozen Roses*...'

Alfred Seaborn? Or *Alfred R. Kinleyside* and *Sea* Blue Publishing House? How blind I was!

'Why did you think it is?' I couldn't hide my excitement.

'They are very similar characters' explained Mr Cartwright. 'A charming guy with an extremely selfish personality... *Rifkin* liked to terrorize women psychologically, and *Seaborn* physically abused them. A strong, smart female character defeats both. *Rifkin* was arrested, and *Seaborn* died in a car accident while fleeing.'

I didn't remember *Seaborn* well; so I had to refresh my knowledge. Where is the library?

■—■—■—■□■—■—■—■

Rifkin didn't do anything for which you can be held accountable. If Mr Cartwright was right, *Seaborn* did it. So, I didn't have any time to philosophize about whether other people thought it was strange or not. I wanted to know; I must know.

135

There was a legal deposit, brand new. I thought that I was the first person who opened it—and the librarian when she sealed it in. I concentrated on the parts in which *Seabond* also appeared. Miss Evans hated that guy—that was pretty obvious. *Seabond* was just a minor character, a disgusting man. He raped a young woman somewhere in the chapter three. I supposed that would be the motivation. Miss Evans' first novel, which had been written about Kinleyside, was just a sketch. The second one showed his real face. Six years passed between the publications of her two books. Perhaps Miss Evans had spent that time searching every dirty thing about Kinleyside.

While I was walking home, I passed by Miss Evans' bookshop. Not by chance, but I brought a white rose. As Mr Cartwright said, there were many colourful flowers, dozens of candles, a few photos and drawings. The images were taken in her bookshop, with students, readers and authors perhaps smiling happily. I didn't recognize anybody. I just stood in front of the flowers for minutes as if I hoped they would answer my question; after that, I placed a rose among the others.

'Emily was a great personality' a female voice suddenly spoke. 'She was so kind, helpful...'

I slowly turned towards the voice.

That woman was thirty or thirty-five years old, thin and pale. She wore light, cheerful pattern clothes with enormous triangles, circles and squares, but her eyes were sad.

'I went to her book club' started I. 'She was amazing. I learned a lot from Miss Evans.'

Then, a very strange thing happened. That woman kindly smiled at me.

'Emily could heal the wound of the heart' said she.

Also, I'm not too proud of what happened either. We started to talk, and I played a broken-hearted man who lost everything: his job and his wife. I know I cheated to get information.

I invited her for a coffee. She was very communicative after listening to my suffering. She wrote poems, and Miss Evans had helped to search for a publisher a year ago. They were friends and talked a lot about art, poets, poems, and other things. I suspected she had a secret, a big, sad secret.

'This is my book' she showed me on your phone screen very proudly. 'This is the best thing that has happened to me for years. You know...'

I got it!

'You don't have to talk about it if you don't...' I whispered.

'Emily always said me... she said... I have to face my fear.'

'Emily was right, I think.'

'I think so... I had to face my fear' she took a deep breath. 'Ten years ago, I met someone... I had some poems and he suggested that I send them to a few addresses... I thought we were friends, but one night he came to me... Sorry, it's too hard...'

'I know' I nodded because I didn't want to torture her.

'Emily wrote the whole story in her novel, and that ugly creature died in it. I was happy... I'm happy now. It is a bad thing, isn't it?' she looked at me, frightened.

'No, it isn't. That was the only way to get rid of him. If I guess, well, you are one of the *Frozen Roses*.'

'That's right… you know her book was published a month ago, and since then, it's like I've been liberated.'

'A month ago?' I asked involuntarily.

'Yes. There was also a small celebration in her bookshop.'

A month ago… I solved the puzzle.

In 2018, at the London Book Fair, Miss Evans met a man. Their romance lasted a few months. Miss Evans was a wise woman. She quickly recognized that man's nature. She wrote about her bad romance and experiences in a novel. About a year ago, Miss Evans realized that her earlier lover had raped a young woman. Miss Evans took revenge in her way. Kinleyside read her new book—I think he read every Stanley Phillips novel with fear. He visited Miss Evans, argued, Kinleyside lost his self-control, and strangled her. A few seconds later, he recognized what he had done and tried to disguise it as an accident—quite clumsily. He was so lucky that we didn't meet him, and he managed to disappear from the scene. That's all. And what can Harvey do with that? I don't know, but Miss Evans thought that I was a terrible reader but an excellent hunting dog.

TEN

I ORDERED A hundred copies of the poetry book. I decided to support the author, and I had many Christmas gifts. Courier service sent a message: *The package will arrive within an hour.*

Somebody rang.

I hurried to the door and opened it. Nobody stood in the corridor, but I found a copy of *The Times*—a current one. When I scanned the newspaper, a postcard fell on the carpet. The photo depicted Nelson's Column in Trafalgar Square, London. It was not posted. My unknown friend only wrote: *Thank you.* That was Harvey, who loved to send postcards—to Miss Evans also. I thought he talked with Mr Ross—Admiral Nelson appeared too many times, it couldn't be a coincidence. Perhaps Miss Evans left an encrypted note to him.

Very funny, Harvey!

I continued to read *The Times*. At first, it seemed like there was nothing worthwhile in it. Then I found an obituary... obituary of Alfred R. Kinleyside, who died in a car accident.

What can I say? I would not like to be Harvey's enemy.

PART III

Country Life

ONE

IT WAS RAINING. Of course, it was raining as I was driving somewhere in Norfolk—especially near Norwich. A moving company transported my belongings. They promised to arrive on Saturday. But that boring Monday, I had an official visit to my superior, Chief Superintendent Lewis T. Farrell, but I was late 'cause of the rain.

Two weeks ago, I bought an old, worn blue Mini Cooper—the blue siren looks good on it. That morning, I packed the most essential things on the back seats like Lady Worsley's portrait, my laptop, some books, Mr Brown's boxes of cookies as if I were preparing for a South Pole expedition, Mrs Alford's gift—champagne, what else—and the others. I started very early, about 6 am, and I hoped to be in Norwich before 11 am—that was my appointment with Farrell at 11 am on Monday.

My Mini Cooper stopped near the imposing brick building at 10:55. I knew well it wasn't a good omen if you're late at the first time. I was in uniform, didn't need to explain, and a young constable guided me. At 11:02, I entered my new superior's office, and I suddenly had a feeling of *déjà vu*.

'Finally! You're two minutes late' started Farrell. He was a great guy, measured in pounds, not brainpower. 'It doesn't surprise me, you know. Superintendent Laverton already drew my attention.'

Wonderful. I started with a clean slate, didn't I?

After that, he spoke for twenty minutes about his beloved wife, Honoria; that was the briefing.

'Dismissed!' he waved nervously, and I think he was a little relieved—our cooperation may not be smooth.

I was relieved, too, because the game rules were clean, even if not pleasant.

∎—∎—∎—∎▢∎—∎—∎—∎

I drove out of Norwich, and about fifteen minutes later, I passed through Poringland and turned right. I didn't move even a mile when it didn't rain, but it was pouring rain. I had to pull over on the side of the road. I couldn't see anything, and the windscreen wipers didn't help in that situation. I waited for a few minutes... and more... and more. I completed that twelve-minute journey in an hour and a half. Despite all those things, I decided to concentrate on the positive aspects.

The police station was in the centre, between the Catholic church and Mrs Matthews' general store. My Mini parked near the entrance, but I got wet in that heavenly blessing. I entered and looked around.

Opposite the door stood the counter behind which an older, stocky man was dozing in a sergeant's uniform. He wore a small dark moustache. I didn't have to worry about waking him up. He didn't even hear it when I rang the bell on the counter. Above the sergeant's head hung a full-length portrait of Queen Elisabeth II. That also showed how the time passed there. Next to Her Majesty, a photo of Princess Diana was placed, accompanied by a black ribbon, in the right corner.

At the next moment, a young policeman appeared with a teapot in his hand. He had big floppy ears and a childish face. The sound of the bell had lured him out.

'Chief Inspector Morgan' remarked he in surprise. 'Sir!' he saluted quickly. 'Chief Superintendent Farrell informed me that you'll arrive just tomorrow morning, Sir' explained he. 'If I had known...'

'No problem, Constable. What's your name?'

'James Stevenson, Sir.'

'Continue the started operation, Stevenson' ordered I.

While the young Constable made the tea, I was walking around the rooms—if I were in *Thomas and Friends*. We had a small kitchen and toilets, a narrow corridor, three small cells, a miniature office, and a room used as a warehouse. Yellowed curtains on the window, some wilting flowers and plants, spider webs everywhere. It seemed I also saw a little mouse.

'It's a great honour to work with you, Sir,' Stevenson said, handing me a cup of tea. I felt like he was speaking honestly.

I didn't know what I could say. Instead of answering, I'd rather go out for a box of Mr Brown's tasty cookies. When I opened the box, the sleeping sergeant suddenly woke up.

'Lemon with almond' noticed he with a smile. 'Ah, Chief Inspector, are you here? I hope Constable Stevenson showed everything.'

The young policeman turned red. He lacked the sergeant's self-confidence.

'Yes, he did, Sergeant Taylor' I answered. By then, I already knew his name.

So, three of us were the whole staff of the Lower Oaks Police Station.

After the tea, Stevenson informed me of the actual cases. Someone stole the poor box from the Catholic church, and that Sunday was the charity fair. At first, I hoped that he mentioned it because the old ladies regularly fought over the cakes, but he started to laugh and explained to me that the Police Station also had a table. We had to make some sweetmeats—that was Chief Superintendent Farrell's order. I felt like there was enough excitement today.

It rained nonstop. That was a calm and quiet afternoon. Stevenson and I cleaned my office while I interrogated him. Punctually, I asked some questions about that town. I planned to visit the superior of Lower Oak the next day. Stevenson gave me the list, but he noticed it was easy to do. So there was the Mayor, Oscar Hampton, and his older brother, Reverend Thomas Hampton, an Anglican priest. After that, his youngest brother, Jacob Hampton, the lawyer, and their brother-in-law, Doctor Adam Stemming, found that formality was very important to them. Stevenson also spoke about Father Wilson from the Catholic church, who was a cheerful and good-natured fellow. The young Constable suggested that I start with the three Hamptons, after the Doctor, and finally Father Wilson. That seemed reasonable.

I already knew that Stevenson's father was a policeman and had died ten years ago in Norwich. He had been shot during a night patrol. Stevenson and his mother lived in Lower Oak for three years, and he passed his exams last year. Sergeant Richard Taylor has slept there for many years; nobody knew how many years he had been there, but he had eleven months until his retirement. He had a lovely wife and three children.

By the way, I think Stevenson was very enthusiastic, and behind the counter was the best place for Sergeant Taylor.

The young Stevenson navigated me to find my new home because I couldn't see anything in that rain, and I didn't know that town yet.

Its name was Rhubarb House. Stevenson said the garden was full of that plant—practically indestructible. I remembered something that Mr Brown said about the rhubarb jam or pie.

'My mom used to make compote from it' explained the young Stevenson. 'That's it, Sir!' He pointed to a small brick house covered in ivy. The fence and the whole garden looked like a wild land in Wales.

I tried to notice the route because I took Stevenson home by car—although he wanted to walk so heroically in the rain. Lower Oak was a small town, with a population of approximately 930, according to 2023 data. So if you're lost, it won't be a tragedy. Only twenty minutes and I found the Rhubarb House again.

My Mini Cooper was parked next to the rusty gate decorated with ivy. I fought with the lock and the lush vegetation for minutes before I could open it. I had an easier time with the door. The rooms were empty and lifeless. Fortunately, in the kitchen was a gas stove and kitchen cabinet, and they had left a great bed upstairs. I wanted nothing more than a cup of tea with lemon and rum and a hot bath. Thus, I brought my stuff into the house.

Tea and bath. The tea was the most important and first thing. I entered the kitchen, and I turned the tap. At first, a burnished liquid began to flow, which smelled of iron and mud. A few minutes later, it was clean; it looked drinkable in terms of taste, smell, and colour. I boiled the water for five minutes. And finally, my tea with rum was fitting for the occasion. With the mug in hand, I went upstairs to check out the bathroom.

The same thing happened to the water as in the kitchen, but the electric boiler was definitely dead. I had to compromise and settle for a lukewarm bath instead of my dream hot bath. I found two huge cooking pots. I boiled the water in them. My grandma told me that during the war, they often heated the water that way. It was not a very modern method, but it suited Rhubarb House and the whole Lower Oak—I think—and I liked it.

Lady Worsley's portrait was on the dreary wall of the bedroom. When I hung it on the angle, I knew it wouldn't be hard to wake up on time. I got no sleep; just tossed and turned all night and heard the dance of raindrops on the windowsill.

TWO

IT WAS STILL raining, and the sky was a dirty grey. Stevenson said that weather could take up to four or five days. Wonderful. That was Lower Oak's welcome drink.

Sergeant Taylor saluted between eating two biscuits and nodded whenever I told him. After an uninformative briefing, Constable Stevenson and I began my introductory visit. The City Hall was a modern, new construction four-story building, but it didn't fit in with the rest of the town and towering over a man like Doctor Frankenstein's monster made of glass and steel. We were already stopped on the ground floor at the reception desk. A few minutes later, a nice, elegant, but cold woman tiptoed towards us.

'Mayor Hampton sends a message to you.' She started wearing pearly pink lipstick and looked like she was giving a speech practice, too articulate. 'If he needs your assistance, he'll call you. He's so busy. Please, do not disturb him.' She made a smile as a point at the end.

'Thank you kindly, *Mme*.' That was my joke because I knew well she preferred *Miss*. Mutually disappointed, we parted without a word.

Our next station was Thomas Hampton's office—the great lawyer. We have made definite progress and reached the door of the second level. Hampton's assistant, an ambitious young man, informed us that the lawyer had travelled to London. Still, if he were there, we couldn't talk to him, except that we had an official assignment. The assistant was very polite and promised to convey our greetings to him.

2:0. We didn't perform well.

On the other hand, Reverend Jacob Hampton was at home and invited us to his library. He sat at his beautiful Victorian oak writing desk, and we stood as two schoolboys in front of the director.

'What can I do for you, gentlemen?' asked he with curiosity.

'I would like to introduce myself, Reverend Hampton' started I.

'Oh, yes! I know. Superintendent Farrell called me yesterday.'

In that case, I didn't have much to say.

Six minutes and seventeen seconds. We sent six minutes and seventeen seconds in the vicarage—I measured it. And twenty-five in the waiting room of Doctor Stemming.

His assistant looked like a Valkyrie of Richard Wagner, a determined plump woman in blue carrying a bedpan as a lance. Sorry, I imagined the bedpan; in reality, she was holding a folder in her hand. She looked at me, felt sorry and immediately led me into the consulting room—advantage of my left burnt face.

'What is your complaint?' Doctor Stemming didn't even look at me, just stood at the medicine cabinet and arranged the bottles on the shelves.

'I'm the new Chief Inspector, Doctor.'

'And?'

'I think we cooperate…'

'Cooperate? What do you mean?' He suddenly turned to me and became angry.

'I mean, if we had a body… a dead body…'

'I see' he sighed with relief. 'Look. There hasn't been any bloody dead body here since 1946. Lower Oak is a very peaceful town. Otherwise, if you find one, I had to call Norwich. So I don't think we should cooperate. That's all? If yes, please send the next patient.'

I sent him.

By the way, I checked that information later, and according to the official statistics, the last murder happened in 1946. An American Corporal shot a local man—the cause had been jelousy. The Corporal had been acquitted because the man had attacked him with a pitchfork.

2:2 in the context of personal meeting, and 4:0 in the context of cooperation. Depressing like the weather, indeed. But the next moment, I saw *Caffé Napoli*. I think that place was a stranger in Lower Oak than I. So I must go in there.

'*Buongiorno, Commisarrio!* That was a very warm welcome.

'*Buongiorno, Padrone!*' That was my warm answer and an essential part of my Italian knowledge.

We shook hands as old friends.

Il Padrone was a potty, optimistic fellow in white cook's jacket and black trousers. He wore a red kerchief on his neck, and he had a wide smile with a thousand teeth and dark brown hair.

After the greeting, I looked around thoroughly. There were some customers, old ladies, a woman with three little children, and two grey-haired men at the corner. Red checkered tablecloths with a red rose in a vase, carved chairs, and the pleasant smell of coffee—as we were in Naples. I had plenty of time because *Il Padrone* cheerfully explained something in Italian, assuming I understood. Although I managed to filter only one word:

'*...mangiare...*'

'*Si, mangiare*' nodded I.

A satisfied smile appeared on his face, and he dragged us—Stevenson and I—to the table next to the counter. He decided what we would eat, and a few minutes later, he served us his special menu.

'*Pizzetta Margharita...* after *Pistacchiosa e Caffé Napoletano...*'

Shame or not, I devoured all of them, and as I noticed, Stevenson didn't need much convincing, either. Mr Rotunno—Stevenson informed me about his name—didn't want to allow paying. Finally, I fought a draw: I paid the bill, but he packed us some delicious cheesecakes as a gift.

I probably won't spend much time in Lower Oak, but I want to spend a lot of time in *Caffé Napoli.*

■—■—■—■□■—■—■—■

When we arrived at the Police Station, I found a strange, tall and broad-shouldered man in the kitchen. He was a head and a half taller than I, and he was making tea, wearing a black cassock and pretending to be at home.

'That's Father Wilson' whispered Stevenson.

'Nice to meet you, Chief Inspector!' saluted Wilson. 'I'm afraid we haven't met yet.' He put down the tea box. 'Brian Wilson… I mean Father Wilson…'

I didn't understand that situation. Would he have been jovial with that salutation? But his movements were somewhat military, and I later noticed that he also had a limp. At first sight, I might have thought he was a member of some kind of force, not a priest.

'Nice to meet you, Father Wilson.' We shook hands, and I felt his strong handshake. 'If I guess well, you already know my name.'

Wilson nodded with a smile and continued tea-making.

'You know' he said 'Lower Oak is a very little town. When we learned that Rhubarb House had a new tenant, we were thrilled. Not much happens around here.'

I think so.

'So, Father, as for the poor box…'

'That's exactly what I came' he explained and poured the boiled water in the teapot. 'I would like to withdraw the complaint… The Bishop insisted on… but I think that poor man needed it so much… Otherwise, there couldn't have been any money in it—perhaps about twenty or twenty-five pounds. I hope I didn't cause trouble.'

We haven't invested too much energy in solving the case that wasn't a problem.

'No, you didn't' I answered, took out my wallet and gave him thirty pounds.

'You're very kind, Chief Inspector. Thanks, in the name of the Catholic Church and the congregation of Lower Oak' he said and pocketed the money. 'Are you an Atheist?'

'Anglican, but I'm not a fan of ceremonies.'

'Forgive me, I just asked… a police officer from a distant city… usually… You know…' He smiled again. 'Even though you don't like the ceremonies, I would like to invite you for Sunday Mass at 8 am.'

'I'm thinking about it.'

'That's enough for me.'

Finally, we sat in my office sipping tea with rum.

'You have good taste' said Wilson about the rum, of course. 'In the rainy weather, this kind of warm drink only helps us.'

'How many more days can it last? This weather, I mean.'

'Tomorrow the sun will shine.'

'How do you know that?'

'Can you hear?'

I tried to do it, but I couldn't hear anything.

'It's raining even harder now' explained he. 'It will awaken soon. I have lived here for six years. I know the rain in Lower Oak. Any question?'

'Have you ever met with the Hamptons?'

'That's the VIP section. I'm an insignificant, unimportant person, and they never give me an invitation card' answered Wilson, and poured more rum in his tea. He didn't seem angry or hurt about it, but found it amusing.

'For six years?'

'Yes.'

Then I have no chance.

■—■—■—■☐■—■—■—■

'Chief Inspector...' said the young Stevenson timidly. It was about 4 pm, and I was browsing the file of the last two years sitting at my desk. There was a laptop and printer somewhere—our official equipment—, but I haven't found them yet. Stevenson paced up and down the corridor for minutes, and finally, he gathered the courage to speak, knocked and entered. 'My mom... So... My mom wants to invite you for dinner.' He looked at me pleadingly. 'Last night she scolded me for letting you just walk away.'

I knew that family dinner. They finished with awkward silence or artificially polite conversation. I also knew well that invitation was unavoidable.

'You're very kind, thank you' I nodded, starting my artificially polite conversation.

'I appreciate, Sir. Thank you! I'll call her right away' smiled Stevenson.

I was not so enthusiastic.

When we walked out the door, it was still raining. The weather didn't help us in determining the time of day.

As a guest, I would like to bring a gift, and since I couldn't think of anything better, I bought a lilac orchid. Stevenson told me that his mother adored the flowers.

My Mini Cooper was parked a little further. We had to hurry so as not to get wet. I rang and waited. As a matter of fact, I expected a short, thin, sad-eyed woman in black, as you imagine a widow. But a red-haired ruddy woman opened the door. She wore a pink body-hugging pullover and tight jeans. Her makeup was heavy for the time of day and the weather—or she wanted to offset the rainy days' feeling.

'Come in!' cried she happily. 'The dinner is ready.'

She led us through a narrow corridor. The walls were covered by photographs and postcards. I recognised the young Stevenson as a baby, as a child and finally in uniform. There were some photos about the late Stevenson, too, and a new guy.

'My name is Shirley' Mrs Stevenson explained. 'And this is my second husband, Doug.'

When I entered the dining room, which was the kitchen too, I saw a middle-aged man sitting at the table. Mrs Stevenson's taste was so pinky and rosy—in the kitchen at all events. A few minutes later, we were done with the introduction, and the orchid was placed in the wide windowsill between a cactus and a geranium.

'Sorry, I'm not a great cook, and hope you like the mirelite dishes' said she, and stepped to the electric oven.

'Don't worry, Mme. I'm a cop and eat everything what is on my plate' answered I.

'Please, call me Shirley. If you say *Mme*, I feel myself old and honourable. Only Shirley. Right, Sean?'

'Right.'

'So, Sean, I think you need a haircut' noted Shirley, opening the oven's door.

'Shirley is the best hairdresser and barber in the world' stated Doug. 'You know, we met in the barber shop where she works. It was love at first sight.'

'Yes, but I insisted that he stop wearing a beard.' Shirley started to laugh. 'Lasagna. Tastier than it looks. The dessert is from the *Caffé Napoli*.'

That was the point when I felt that despite all our differences, Shirley and I still had something in common.

THREE

AS WILSON SAID, at 2 am, the rain stopped. The next thing I remembered was the voice of the alarm clock.

Mud was everywhere, but I ran a tour in military boots that I had bought in a flea market many years ago. Lower Oak was different in sunlight than in the rain. As if the grey drowsiness disappeared, and its colours have come alive.

I ran past the Wilson's house; he was feeding a one-eyed, shaggy tabby cat. We waved to each other. A few minutes later, Doug's car passed me, then suddenly it slowed down.

'Instead of me too' cried he happily through the rolled-down window.

Doug worked at Norwich Railway Station in the office. Last night he told me that he decided to do some sports every day, but somehow it falls short. If he wants, I can also run a tour for him. No problem.

Somewhere, through an open window, I heard a popular jazz song: *It's a new dawn, it's a new day, it's a life for me, and I'm feeling good...* All right then!

That day I went on foot to the Police Station—just a twenty-minute walk. I was the first, and when I opened the entrance, I immediately heard the phone ring. That was an old-time TAM from the 1990s—by the way, the last two days it was mute, but that morning screamed quite loudly.

'Lower Oak Police Station, it's Chief Inspector Morgan. What can I do for you?'

'Thanks God!' said a young man's voice. 'My name is Toby Locke, Sir. My friends and I are camping in the woods about six miles away from Lower Oak, and we find human bones.'

'Tell him about the skull' cried somebody else from a distance.

'A human skull, Sir…' repeated he.

Sergeant Taylor stayed in the station. Stevenson and I took a little trip in my Mini Cooper.

Toby Locke—a pale guy in colourful clothes, with a beard and dreadlocks—was waiting for us by the side of the road. He was scared perhaps because of the skull or the smoked marijuana cigarette—the smell of which could still be on his coat.

'We didn't touch it' started he. 'The guys are totally blocked.'

I nodded and didn't mention the Cannabis Law. Otherwise, we didn't have any empty cells to close Locke and all of his friends.

The skull looked out under a bush with its big, dark orbits. It was dirty white and had been there for years.

Locke said to me once again how he found that bizarre *memento mori* and repeated many times: *We didn't touch it.* I think, despite using mind-altering drugs, he wanted to stay in the world of the living. The young Stevenson noted their data; meanwhile, I called Doctor Stemming. I didn't tell him that was just a skull; rather, I named *the body*. I had a feeling it would pique his curiosity more in that way. Finally, I sent Locke from my crime scene. He seemed grateful that they could disappear quickly.

Doctor Stemming arrived an hour later. I didn't want to move the scene until he saw it. So we stood guard by the bush. Stevenson tried to prove to me how it was exciting, but he was white and didn't dare to look at our special find. A few minutes later, I sent him back to the car.

I had many times. So I thought I was lucky that Locke found the skull, a strange person who called the police immediately. I could imagine some of the local people had seen and known it, but they didn't want to spoil the statistics.

At first, I heard Stevenson's voice. He explained in detail that tourists explored the body, as I had asked him before. Doctor Stemming didn't answer and looked annoyed. He murmured that I had turned upside down his whole day.

'Where is your *body*?' he asked irritably when he noticed me.

'There' I pointed under the bush.

'That is? I hope that is a bad joke' he said angrily.

'That's not a joke, Doctor Stemming, that's a skull.'

'I know that is a skull. Don't educate me, Morgan! How dare you?'

'With respect, Doctor, but...'

'I don't care. I'm so busy and I don't have any time for skulls or other bones. I'm a doctor, not an archaeologist. Call Norwich, not me! And as the German says: *auf Wiedensehen nicht!* He turned his back and hurried away.

That was my plan B: to call the Norwich Police. Things initially went quite well. I managed to catch a very accommodating Inspector. After a brief exchange of information, I had to wait some minutes.

'Terrible sorry, Sir...' he started unexpectedly. 'Chief Superintendent Farrell messaged you that we have many fresh bodies, so my specialists cannot deal with this matter. And the Chief Superintendent said: *This is your district, your jurisdiction.*'

Thank you.

So I had a skull, nothing else.

Then I thought Doctor Robertson. I took some photos with my phone and sent them to him. A few minutes later, I called him.

'I cannot speak...' his voice was muffled. 'I'll call you later...'

'Who's it, Doctor?' That was Professor Grant in the background, the old mummy as Robertson named him.

The line was broken.

I thought for a few seconds about what to do. After that, I sent the young Stevenson to bring a spade and other equipment for the *corpse desecration,* such as gloves, bags and a huge box for the evidence, measuring rods, marking sticks and so on.

I was alone in the forest. I usually like that feeling: a little scary, but also fascinating. I had plenty of time to plan the exploration: I had to dig around the bush and check the neighbourhood. I was sure the victim had been murdered elsewhere, and they had hidden the body in there. That brush may have grown since that time. Perhaps a fox or a stray dog scraped the bones. I tried to organise and note every detail, but my phone started to ring. That was Robertson.

'We'll be there in two hours, and the Professor says: don't touch anything' he instructed me aloud. After that, he continued whispering: 'I'll explain everything.'

I didn't ask any questions. I was satisfied having the best pathologists.

■—■—■—■☐■—■—■—■

Father Wilson arrived first with a spade. One of his congregation took him to the point which Stevenson marked with a cross made of branches. Wilson was searching me at the Police Station when the young Stevenson entered. The Father questioned him thoroughly, and he thought it best to come straight here. There was not a spade among the instruments of the Police Station, but the Father had one and had another reason, too.

'I must fulfil my duty' he said when he stepped next to me and pressed the spade into my hand. He knelt, took some kind of ribbon from his pocket, kissed it and began to pray.

When he finished, he looked at me.

'Help me stand up, please. My knee is stuck.'

I didn't understand what he wanted to tell me, but I pulled him as much as I could.

'My right leg, you know, partly it stayed in Iraq. Pressure mine' he smiled.

'You were a Camp Chaplain, weren't you?'

'No. I was a Lieutenant from the Royal Academy with great ambition and two legs. And now this is my new career' he pointed to the cassock.

I didn't know how to respond. That topic was familiarly awkward. Fortunately, the young Stevenson hurried towards us carrying a huge box and bags. I informed him of the new situation and sent him again, but that time to the *Caffé Napoli* for lunch and dessert—thinking of sweet-toothed Robertson.

After a little pause, Wilson started to speak about the rehabilitation and a Jesuit priest who had visited the patient in the military hospital.

'I had a very beautiful decoration, a silver coloured medal, and they promised a new position in a nice office, but I would have been capable of... You know. I needed something different. I chose that one, and have a Georgian desk now full of woodworm holes, but I have not had to assist sending my comrades to the death.'

I understood, so I nodded.

Many years ago, some fanatics had broken into the Police Station, taken hostages, but a callow constable had fought them. He had been shot twice in his stomach. I had tried to stop the bleeding, but he had been dying when the paramedics had arrived. Watching somebody die and you cannot do anything… It's like you would be the murderer… your hands are soaked in blood, and you can never clean them. When I think about it, I voluntarily look at my hand… I look at the dried blood.

A cold shiver ran down my spine.

'And you, Chief Inspector?' Wilson's voice pulled back into reality.

'Have I to confess, Father?' I wanted to answer with a joke. I hoped he didn't behold my weakness.

'Not necessary, my Son… maybe later.'

'Maybe.'

'All right then… let's talk about poor Yorick's skull. What do you think?'

I preferred that theme. A lively conversation ensued between us about the deceased. We have many ideas, although we didn't know yet what he or she was.

▪—▪—▪—▪□▪—▪—▪—▪

Professor Grant began the work in his meticulous way. From that point on, everything went smoothly. While the two doctors had lunch, I dug a great hole and Wilson took pics with my phone. Stevenson was too pale and was waiting a little further. In summary—and at the end of the excavation—, there were the skull, most of the ribs with animal teeth marks, the pelvic bone and the limbs, but several phalanxes were missing. Robertson found some rusty pieces of metal, and a little further an unidentified rag.

'I think' noticed Professor Grant 'the victim was a young woman.'

'The pelvic bone' explained Robertson.

'And how long…?' I asked carefully.

'At this moment, I would say for four years or more. Maybe in a few days I'll define more exactly the time of the death.'

'I'm very appreciative of your help, Professor.'

'Not at all, Chief Inspector. I'm happy to assist you.'

Honestly, I didn't quite understand why the usually stern Grant was so nice. Robertson explained to me later. A month ago, Robertson had talked to him about my private investigation. Grant had been cheering for my idea, so Miss Evans had been murdered, because both of them had thought Chief Inspector Wallace's scarf theory had been stupid. In Robertson's interpretation, I had been punished for that—I mean for disturbing Wallace. Grant had stated that Wallace was totally incompetent, and Wallace regularly harassed the Professor as that morning. When I sent the photos to Robertson, they were arguing, rather shouting, in Grant's office. That motivated the Professor… and the scientific interest—obviously.

▪–▪–▪–▪◻▪–▪–▪–▪

We finished the fieldwork—that day—and returned to the Police Station. Sergeant Taylor was having tea; he just waved at us. Wilson and I agreed to continue the search in the forest the next day. I thought we needed a few hours to seek. Perhaps we found some evidence or traces—it was practically impossible, but who knows?

Stevenson was disgusted by skulls, bones and—I was sure—the bodies too. So I ordered him another type of inquiry, but first we had to find our official laptop. After two hours of searching, I suspended that operation—we even tidied up our little warehouse. Taylor was tired of doing nothing, and Stevenson seemed exhausted. I saved them from overtime.

I went into the *Caffé Napoli* on my way home. Also, I wanted to go because it was closed. I read the opening hours with amazement on the door: *Monday to Friday 6:30 am—3:00 pm, Saturday 7:00 am—2 pm.* It was closed in teatime every day. I'm not a typical economist, but it was a very bad idea in the United Kingdom.

At that moment, I saw Mr Rotunno behind the glass door. He smiled and waved, pointing backwards. I went around the building to the kitchen entrance. He was waiting for me.

'*Buongiorno, Commissario!*' said he and suddenly hugged me. He spoke very quickly, but I understood something like *entrare.*

He led me to the kitchen. An old lady in a black dress and white apron packed cakes in white paper boxes with that inscription: *Caffé Napoli Founded in 2005*—written in ornate red letters. I saw three other men who cooked, a young man with a huge bag—he was the delivery boy, I think—, and two young women were at the dishwasher. The old lady just nodded, but the other ones welcomed me with a happy *buongiorno.*

I tried to explicate that I wanted to buy some food for dinner. One of the white chef uniforms spoke English. Finally, I received *spaghetti alle vongole*. Mr Rotunno made it himself.

While watching Mr Rotunno cook my dinner—he was a real artist—I chatted with the young English-speaking chef who told me that the City Hall ordered that peculiar opening hours so as not to distract guests from the local tea house—delivery was possible. By the way, the local tea house's name was *Hampton*. When the young chef mentioned the Hampstons, the old lady quickly crossed herself and said:

'*Camorra.*'

As you noticed, my Italian knowledge is not sophisticated; I don't quote from Dante Alighieri or Petrarca, but I know well those words: *vendetta, omertà, cosa nostra* and *camorra*, of course.

I'm afraid that old lady exactly described what I suspected.

Otherwise, the young chef indicated to me, whispering that his family had to escape from Naples because of *Camorra* in the 1990s.

'I explained to my grandma a thousand times that we're in England, in vain. She doesn't want to understand, she doesn't believe...'

Neither I.

My evening was spent with delicious *spaghetti* and some pistachio cakes after a little investigation. I tried to log in on the website of Norfolk Constabulary, but I didn't have an account. I called them, but the night patrol officer could not help me. He didn't permit, and proposed to call back the next morning.

As the Professor said, the bones have been in the forest for four years or more. I started to search articles about missing women in Norfolk. First in 2021, then. It would be probable that she had not lived there—that was the second search filter.

FOUR

EARLY MORNING, I visited Constable Stevenson. He didn't suspect how busy a day he had. Contact Norwich, asking permission and checking information. He received some names from me; he had to examine them and search for others. Wait for information from Professor Grant, but first find that bloody laptop. I prepared for the worst option, and I gave him mine to use. I saw that he liked those tasks.

My second project was a trip with Wilson and his useful spade.

'Don't worry, I have so much time' said Wilson, sitting on the back seat and drinking hot black coffee from a blue tartan thermos. 'My congregation is small; there were thirty-five people, but in October, thirty-six or thirty-seven. It depends on whether Mrs Connor will have twins or not. Usually I don't have much to do. I don't write the Sunday speech in advance; I improvise and tell about the actualities. I also put up a notice on the board asking to call me if anything happened, and if the Bishop's secretary calls me, bad luck.'

It must have been an odd sight. A Catholic priest in cassock and a police officer in uniform are gardening in the forest. Punctually, Wilson examined the soil and vegetation, and I dug around the bush. As expected, nothing worthwhile came of it.

'Perhaps we can try there, behind the oak trees' I suggested, and buried the hole that I had dug before.

'Do you think they dragged her here from the road?'

'This seems the most likely.'

I picked up the spade and headed for the oaks, Wilson following me. At the next moment, I heard a shot. I grabbed Wilson's arm and pulled him down with me into the undergrowth and mud. There were nine or ten shots, and we were hiding as rabbits.

'A hunting rifle' whispered Wilson. 'It's pretty close.'

Pretty close? It whistled past my ear!

We waited for a few minutes. Nothing. Silence.

'What do you think?' asked I.

'They left, intended as a warning. We bothered them, I'm afraid… Poachers perhaps.'

Or not. Fifty-fifty.

∎—∎—∎—∎▢∎—∎—∎—∎

I was angry, yes! I took Wilson home, went to the station and cleaned my uniform. The young Stevenson mentioned something about the firearms certification on my first day in Lower Oak. Last year, an officer of the City Hall had come to check the database, but Stevenson hadn't found it. Finally, the officer had left a list. Stevenson couldn't tell where the list was because Sergeant Taylor had put it somewhere, and Taylor wasn't capable of bringing back his memories. So I visited the City Hall.

I didn't tell anything to Stevenson, who worked diligently, and it seemed the telephone receiver grew to his ear. Sergeant Taylor… so he slept behind the counter. Don't disturb him!

A few minutes later—my uniform had some inconspicuous wet patches—I entered the monstrous building. As last time, a very polite young woman stopped me at the entrance; however, that day I was less patient and raised my voice, mentioning the Firearms Act, and it had an effect. Finally, a man, who looked like a lawyer, escorted me upstairs.

Mayor Hampton was at a meeting, and I only got to a Deputy Mayor, Mr Gibbens.

'You told something about the Firearms Act… you had to know, there are many people who have a gun with certification, Chief Inspector' said he. 'We often go hunting.'

'I'm very glad you started with this. I wanted to ask a list of their names, and check certifications, their guns and this morning's alibis.' I tried to calm down, but I couldn't.

Gibbens seemed tranquil with a cheeky grin on his face.

'Please, don't be ridiculous, Chief Inspector! Just because a few shots were fired in the forest, it doesn't mean that you have to turn the town upside down' he noticed smugly, and he continued to grin unwaveringly.

Wait a moment! I didn't say a word. How did that City Hall baboon know that those shots were in the forest? The response was so simple. Somebody talked to him about the shooting, somebody who was in the forest that morning and maybe that person held the hunting rifle in his hand. Mr Gibbens is doubtless involved in that case… and that phrase: turning upside down. I remembered Doctor Stemming used that.

Fortunately, I had a *bad habit*: in a similar situation, I always used my good manners. Mr Gibbens doesn't have to know what I think.

'You have to understand. Our database is not up-to-date.' I smiled at him—rather, I would have liked to punch him. 'By the way, I didn't receive the firearms certification list from Norwich. I hope we can work together.'

'I informed the Mayor, and I'll call you. That's all I can do.'

It was interesting. Last year, they had released the names without any problem, and when I needed it…

'Thank you, Mr Gibbens… And speaking of the forest. There is a skeleton, as you know. I mean, there was. And we are forced to continue investigating such cases. I hope you don't mind' I spoke with an innocent face, and I was curious how he reacted.

'On the contrary. Do your duty, Chief Inspector' he answered with a calm voice. He didn't seem nervous. As I suspected, they already informed him about the *excavation*. 'But…' Always it was a *but*. 'For the peace of town, the Mayor would like to ask you: no press, no publicity. That was probably an alien. You cannot find anybody who knew' noticed Mr Gibbens.

I translate. Version A—if you informed the press, there will be many shots, and one of them in your head, maybe.

Or version B—that unimportant dead person did not live in our beloved Lower Oak, also it doesn't matter—as you, Chief Inspector Nobody. I think none of them were humane. It would be nice to know which version was correct—just because I ordered lunch or my coffin.

∎–∎–∎–∎☐∎–∎–∎–∎

I needed time to think and took a long walk. When I entered my office, I saw a postcard on my desk. It arrived by post from London—as the stamp testified. It illustrated Big Ben in a watercolour painting. On the back side, there were the Police Station address, my name, rank and a short message: *Congratulations!* Harvey, my secret buddy, sent it. He loved that joke.

But I was in a bad mood. Lower Oak and Miss Unknown's skull, the whole investigation seemed totally hopeless for a moment. At least Harvey was having fun. I would like to invite him to my forthcoming funeral—that case or the boredom kills me—, but I didn't know his address. Perhaps I will post an ad in *The Times* as last time.

Stevenson's appearance abolished my lamentation.

'Sir...'

'Yes?'

'Sir... So...' He started with difficulty.

'Is there any problem?'

Any? Many!

Norwich didn't give permission to my private laptop, only the official one, but Stevenson didn't excavate that equipment—nor did Taylor. We had to fill out a form to declare the absence of the previous one, and another form to request a new one. However, we didn't have any computer, similar thing or printer. Practically, we weren't capable of doing anything, including filling a form. And if we were to send it, then just a few weeks later, they considered the application. Just a few weeks. Wonderful!

'Terrible sorry, Sir...' Stevenson was confused, and I was sure he did everything he could do.

'Don't take it to heart, Constable. Courage. We need a new strategy' said I.

'You know... My cousin works at Poringland Police Station... I called him, and he'll send a few cases. My stepfather will bring them in the evening. I asked him to pick them on his way home... and the forms, of course.'

'Very good, Constable. Your ingenuity saved us... Tomorrow we'll fill those bloody forms and send them to the blockheads in Norwich.' I felt better. 'And say thank you for your stepfather also in my name, please.'

A long time ago, people believed that the radio destroyed the newspaper; after that, they believed the TV destroyed the radio. Now we have newspapers, many radio stations and TV channels. Japanese people read printed manga and papers, yet not only online. Then Lower Oak deserves a chance, I think.

Doctor Robertson called us about 3 pm. He could clarify the age of the victim—he was twenty or twenty-five years old—, but the time of death, unfortunately, could not. Her height was approximately five feet and four or five inches. The cause of death was likely a blow to the back of the head. There was a skull injury. Robertson also said the body had been cut with a special hacksaw, which was similar to the one the surgeons used. That instrument left characteristic imprints on the bone tissues.

At that point, I thought of Doctor Stemming—I knew why perfectly well.

So, we knew the victim was a twenty or twenty-five-year-old young woman, who was knocked down about four years ago, and then they had sliced the body and hidden it in the forest. Robertson promised me to create a portrait based on the skull, but he needed a few days. Things were moving slowly, but moving.

Apropos, all morning and early afternoon, Stevenson spent his time fighting with bureaucracy; consequently, he didn't check the articles about the missing women. Punctually, we could verify two names on that list yet. One of them died last year and was buried in the local cemetery; the other one had gone home a few months after she went missing.

■—■—■—■□■—■—■—■

After receiving those files from Poringland, I went home. I planned to check them alone, but Father Wilson arrived with meat pies—I suspect he bought them in Mrs Matthew's general store. That was just right because I wanted to talk to him anyway.

'I haven't notified the Bishop yet about the body' started Wilson. We stood at the kitchen counter and ate. I didn't have chairs yet; they arrive on Saturday. 'He's a little bit nervous... I mean sensitive, you know. But I thought a lot... Poor young woman... I pray for her...And... you have to investigate what happened to her.'

'Yes, I know. We already have a few names' I replied after swallowing the thoroughly chewed morsel. 'If we could identify her, we could get closer to the solution.'

'I help if I can. Maybe she was a Catholic...'

I saw Wilson was truly shaken.

'Maybe, and... Terrible sorry about the shooting, Father Wilson' I apologised. Risking my life is one thing, but I wouldn't risk the life of anybody else.

'Never mind. I have to admit I even found it exciting' smiled he. 'Do you know who shot us?'

I nodded.

'The murderer?'

I didn't give any answer.

'Or his accomplice?... Don't worry. I also know the confidentiality.'

I hesitated for a few moments.

'So... In my opinion... they wanted to scare us' I told him what Mr Gibbens said to me and my conjecture.

'Right. After all, this is a kind of proof. They knew the body, and I think they knew the victim who had been' nodded

Wilson. 'This is good and bad... I mean good because you know where to search for the murderer, but bad because they had some kind of power. You must be very prudent, Chief Inspector.'

As usual.

But it could be that Wilson was half right, and they knew the body, but didn't know who was... No. Unfortunately, I felt more and more that they knew everything and only played with me.

FIVE

THE NEXT DAY brought no change either. As if everybody is preparing for the big Sunday charity fair. As a matter of fact, some little things happened. For example, an old lady reported her missing cat by phone. Stevenson found it on a branch of an oak tree. We caught a bicycle thief, there was a broken window in the local pub, and some kids painted a great FUCK subtitle on the wall of the Catholic church with poop brown oil paint. That was the country life on Friday.

Last night I hid the missing people's files in one of the kitchen cabinets' drawers. I thought they were in a safe place, and I didn't even think about it 'til night. Then I checked them and went to sleep.

On Saturday morning, the moving company's truck stopped in front of the Rhubarb House, and the packing started. The young Stevenson, his family and Father Wilson helped me. For the evening, almost everything fell into place.

Shirley brought four cheese and salami pizzas—frozen, of course—and we ate in my living room.

'Honestly, I'll bake apple pies with vanilla sauce' explained Shirley between two slices of pizza. 'There are many pies left, generally. We'll eat them, but Sergeant Taylor's wife never makes anything… I think Taylor devours every sweetmeat. And you, Sean?'

I didn't understand the question.

'Tomorrow, the charity fair, you know?'

Charity fair? A lot of things were on my mind, but not that.

'Yes?' I asked, confused.

'The Police Station has a table. We traditionally sell cakes' answered Shirley.

Yes! Chief Superintendent Farrell sent a message about that fair. I didn't pay much attention to it, sorry. A skull is still more interesting.

'So we have a table. Right.' I nodded. 'And sell cakes. What kind of cakes?'

Shirley looked at me with an understanding smile.

'I'll bake apple pies, Sean' repeated she. 'Frozen apple pies, you know, with vanilla sauce. It's not fair because the old girls sell cakes too. The *Brockleby's* cannot compete with grandmas.'

But I knew a person who could.

▪—▪—▪—▪□▪—▪—▪—▪

For less religious reasons, finally, I went to Catholic Mass as I wanted to repay Wilson's help. I sat on a bench in the backside. Wilson was right; his congregation was very small. Most of them consisted of the Rotunno family, but there were some Irish or Scottish, red-haired people. Later, I recalled that Wilson mentioned something about a certain Mrs Connor. Then they were Irish, I think.

Wilson's speech took a short time. He talked about the transience of life, the inscrutability of God and the importance of the charity fair. After the Mass, I chatted a little bit with Mr Rotunno and his English-speaking nephew. I introduced myself to the red-haired family, the Connors, and I had to hurry home to make our cakes.

At 2 pm, the Mayor opened the charity fair. I didn't see him, because our table was placed at the back, but I heard his template text. He didn't have original style.

That year, we—I mean the young Stevenson, Shirley, his stepfather and I—made different types of muffins based on Mr Brown's online instructions. He said *even I can do this*. When Mr Brown viewed our finished works, he looked satisfied and proud. He was sure that we won the first prize and asked me to call him later. One type of them we decorated with cream and candied violets. Mr Brown spoke about Elizabeth the First, who had a sweet tooth, and the violets were her favourite. I liked the idea and thought that was extravagant. If I noticed Shirley looked a lot like that Queen, she secretly ate three of them.

At the charity fair, I tried to take advantage of this opportunity and talk to the people, but I didn't have much success. Most of them just walked next to the table. The *old girls* stared, observed our cakes and bought or not. However, Mr Rotunno and his family spent much time with us. We chatted again about foods and drinks, especially pistachio coffee. He was very interested in Elizabeth the First and violets, and brought all of that type of muffin. By the way, Father Wilson visited us several times, and he was a generous customer.

At the end of the fair, we had four pieces of muffins—one for each person. We ate them quickly. As expected, we won no prize. I think the jury didn't walk to the back table. Shirley was a little bit disappointed, but I didn't care that much, because I observed the crowd. I recognised Mr Gibbens and saw Reverend Hampton. Shirley, who met many people in her work, gave me much information about those men. I think she was an excellent observer, knew human nature and summarised her knowledge professionally. In addition, I learned a lot about the types of beard, moustache and wig and had a haircut on Friday evening.

When I returned to the Rhubarb House, I was annoyed that I hadn't made any progress in that case, but I've already learned: *patience brings roses... also traces.*

SIX

ANOTHER MONDAY.

That morning, I had many plans, but after my running tour, I received a call from Poringland. A certain Superintendent Jones ordered me to brief at 9 am. I suspected he could be a friend of Farrell from Norwich. I calculated that my Monday morning was pointless or all day. I informed the young Stevenson and gave him some tasks. Because I had a feeling that my laptop might be needed, I sent Stevenson to Father Wilson, who offered us to use the computer of the Catholic church.

I thought that 9 am was too early. Farrell and similar fellows usually start the daily routine after 10 am. He makes me wait, and I'll be glad that the Superintendent audits me after his lunch.

It was 8:10 when I arrived at the Poringland Police Station. The patrol officer congratulated me for my new position and led me straight to the Superintendent, who was in there and ordered me immediately.

So… Superintendent Jones was about five feet tall, a dark-haired, slim but forceful woman in her forties. She wore a dark pantsuit with a light blue blouse, sitting at her desk and reading something on the screen. She looked strict and a little bit nervous.

'You came early, Chief Inspector. Sit down' she pointed to the chair opposite the table. 'Just a minute.'

I nodded.

When she finished the reading, she looked at me.

'If I know, last Friday you asked for files of missing people. Next time you ask me, not a Corporal. Why didn't you use the official way? It's not regular.' She frowned.

'Terrible sorry, Mme…' started I. If she were a typical rule follower, I could get some help. 'I took over the position last Monday, and at this moment we don't have any equipment. I mean, our infrastructure is incomplete. I would like to fill the form, but we don't have a printer yet.'

She surprised.

'I thought that Poringland is poorly equipped' noticed she. 'You must follow the rules at all times, you know?'

'Yes, Mme.'

'And what's this?'

'My private laptop, Mme.'

'Right. Bring me a cup of coffee and a ham sandwich from the canteen. In the meantime, I'll try to put something for you.'

'Thank you, Mme.'

I left my machine in her office and hurried to the canteen. In the corridor, I met a young sergeant who helped me to find my destination.

'I would like to ask for a coffee for Superintendent Jones and a ham sandwich' I said to the counter, a wrinkled-faced man.

'The usual.' He looked at me for an instant. 'First day, Chief Inspector?'

'No. I came from Lower Oak.'

'That station is closed, isn't it?' He turned towards me suspiciously.

'Not yet. That's my new position.'

'I see' he nodded and continued coffee-making. 'Is old Taylor still there and is he as fast as before?'

I didn't know Taylor had been fast before or not, but I didn't think he would be changed.

'I think so.'

The counter smiled.

I think I had to visit that station more often. The counter was a serviceable database.

When I entered Jones' office, she sat at the desk, but there was another person in there, an Indian man in a suit with glasses. I put the paper cup and the sandwich on the desk.

'Thank you, Chief Inspector. You're very kind' said Jones dryly. 'This is my husband, Rahul Bhatt. He works in the economics department. Rahul, this officer came from Lower Oak, Chief Inspector Sean Morgan.'

'Nice to meet you, Sir.'

'Nice to meet you, Mr Bhatt.'

After a short handshake, Mr Bhatt adjusted his glasses as if embarrassed.

'I explained to Rahul your situation, and he'll see what we can do.' Jones looked at her husband.

'Yes. I'll go and take care of it right away.' And he did… right away.

'Now, Chief Inspector, let's get back to our original topic. You asked for files of missing women, right?'

'Right, Mme.'

'But why?'

I sat down on the chair and searched for the photo of a skull on my laptop. That was more elegant than my phone, I think.

'Last Wednesday, the tourists found it.' I showed the pic to Jones, who became excited. 'She was a twenty or twenty-five-year-old, her height about five feet and four or five inches. They knocked her on the back of her head after they cut the body with an amputation hacksaw or something similar. I suppose they killed her somewhere else, but buried her in the forest.'

'When?'

'Four years ago or even longer.'

'Who is your pathologist?'

'Professor Grant and Doctor Robertson. I'll receive a portrait of the victim in a few days.'

'You have a good connection.' She thought for a few seconds. 'Show me that place, Chief Inspector.'

There is a pleasure in the pathless woods—as Lord Byron wrote. As a matter of fact, we had no pleasure in those twenty minutes wandering, which led us to the crime scene, because the previous day, somebody had taken away the signal cross—intentionally. I'm not a David Attenborough. We found the upturned bush yet. Superintendent Jones looked around thoroughly, and after a short walk, asked me to take her to the Police Station.

Meanwhile, I knew that her total name was Gwen Jones; she had lived and served in Cardiff, but a few years ago moved to Poringland. So she was a Welsh woman with an Indian husband.

I thought it would be pointless to go to the station. There was Sergeant Taylor behind the counter, nothing special. I led her to the parish behind the church.

When Jones entered the room, the young Stevenson stood up and saluted. Father Wilson, too. It was amusing. I think they felt the power of Superintendent Gwen Jones. Stevenson said to us that he cancelled two other names from our list. Jones thanked him and asked for a coffee.

'I'm addicted to caffeine' she confessed.

No problem. I know the perfect place.

'*Buongiorno, Commissario!*' Mr Rotunno greeted and hugged me, and I was not careful enough; he would kiss me, too, on my face.

'*Buongiorno, Padrone!*' I said and introduced the Superintendent.

Mr Rotunno was not interested in British police ranks; for him, Jones was a *bellissima signorina*. He kissed her hand and winked at me with a wide smile. I'll explain the situation to him if necessary.

A few hours later, we closed the day with the following balance. The Poringland Police bought all of the sweetmeats, pizzas and pastas from the *Caffé Napoli.* The Lower Oak Police received a scrapped, but functional computer and printer. By the way, that computer had legal and valid access permission to the database. In return, Jones asked for continuous information. It was a good balance, isn't it?

SEVEN

SHORTLY AFTER MIDNIGHT, Doctor Robertson called me, and then sent the portrait of our mysterious victim. I got dressed and immediately went to the station. I found her within thirty minutes in the database. I alerted Jones, as she asked before.

'Her name is Abby Combe. She was twenty-one years old from Poringland. Her parents reported her missing on July 6, 2019' started I.

'Yes, I'm searching… I got it. Abby Combe was born on December 3, 2002, in Norwich… She lived in Poringland, yes… There is a new note. Her parents requested a further search two weeks ago. We'll visit them in the morning. Can you come here at 7 am, Chief Inspector?'

'Of course, Mme.'

The only question was what I did until then, because I could not sleep. It was sure.

■—■—■—■□■—■—■—■

When my Mini Cooper stopped in front of the Poringland Police Station, I knew everything about the Combes. I mean everything that you can know from the internet. There was much information in my head, but the most important thing was yet to come: the personal meeting.

Mr and Mrs Combe lived in a two-story red brick building. They waited for us because Jones sent a message to them before. Mrs Combe led us to the living room and offered a coffee. We accepted it. She and her daughter looked very much alike: blonde hair, round face, big brown eyes and thin mouth. I think their body shape may also be similar. There was some kind of sadness in Mrs Combe's eyes if she already knew the bad news. Mr Combe just sat in the armchair, smoked; his fingers were yellow from nicotine. The whole room—I mean the furniture, curtains and so on—was neat and clear, just the cigarette didn't fit there. I think Mrs Combe allowed her husband to smoke only that morning.

'Are you bothered by the smoke?' asked Mrs Combe, worried.

'No. Not at all.' answered I.

Jones wanted me to interrogate them; she *only* observed. She said the people preferred the male police officer in that town.

Mrs Combe poured coffee into the cups.

'Sugar? Milk?'

'Just sugar, please.'

A few minutes later, sitting on a sofa and sipping coffee, we stared at each other. Hard thing. Suddenly, I decided. I put the coffee cup on the table—it was like a garbage container had fallen on the asphalt.

'Mr and Mrs Combe, last Wednesday we found your daughter's body...' Understanding that I didn't mentioned the skull. It would be have insensitivity.

'Gosh! Pete! I knew it. I told you' Mrs Combe shouted painfully and started to cry.

Mr Combe didn't say any word, stubbed the cigarette in the ashtray and lit another one.

'My little Abby! Jesus! My little Abby!' repeated Mrs Combe continuously.

I waited for a few seconds, then I asked gently:

'How did you know that, Mrs Combe?'

'I felt it' sobbed she.

Mr Combe lighted another cigarette.

'Where?' he spoke suddenly.

'Near to Lower Oak.'

'Lower Oak?' wondered Mrs Combe. 'Abby didn't know anybody there.' She turned toward her husband. 'Do you hear, Pete? Abby was in Lower Oak. Why did she tell me?'

But Mr Combe already went into a catatonic state and stared blankly ahead.

'I would like to ask some questions, Mme, and if it's possible, look around in her room.' I continued.

Mrs Combe nodded.

It was a dramatic scene. I inspected the girl's room. Her parents left everything so that she could enter at any moment. Before I entered, I stopped for a moment as a respect of the dead girl. She had loved the vivid colour, especially the pink, magenta, lemon and orange yellow. Loved Korean boy bands and Adam Lambert—when he could be a member of a Korean boy band. She had many bijous—most of them worthless plastic—and makeup kits, lipsticks, cheap perfumes and so on.

'Did she write a diary?'

'No' answered Jones. 'When they reported her missing, my colleagues were here and took everything which could be a trace.'

'Yes, it's right' sniffed Mrs Combe. 'They took many things, but I received a certification. I'll bring it right away.'

'Thanks, Mme.'

During waiting, I went to her dressing table. I felt around the back of the table. Nothing. I pulled out the drawer. Nothing. Next, the bed and the wardrobe came.

'I'm here' Mrs Combe said, entering the room again. 'Do you search Abby's secret box?'

I raised my head. Abby had a secret box?

'Your colleague brought it back. A very kind constable.'

'Where is it, Mrs Combe?' At that moment, I felt it was very important. 'May I see it?'

'In bedroom...' She wiped teardrops and hurried.

A few minutes later, she returned with an old wooden box which had a little open lock. Jones and I got out of it and back in, but Abby's secret stuff contained nothing secret: coasters, a dried red rose, a broken bracelet, caps of bottles, an empty cigarette boksz and a Christmas cards. I already understood why the police officer gave it back.

Mr Combe's state changed a little bit. He's talking to somebody by phone. He spoke slowly and quietly. I waved at him, but he didn't look at me. I heard Gwen Jones' voice as she said the official text. We walked across the short hallway to the entrance. Mrs Combe opened the door crying. Jones left the house. I just passed the low cupboard when I saw a dirty pink paper box.

'Do you know that place? Is it good?'

'I've never been there. Abby brought some strawberry cakes in that box. It happened one day before her disappearance. We ate the cakes that evening, but I cannot throw them out. If I look at this box, I remember our last happy time.'

I felt like a bucket of ice had been poured on my neck. *Hampton Tea House...* one day before her disappearance.

'What do you think, Chief Inspector?' asked Gwen Jones after leaving the Combes' house.

A cake box was not evidence I knew and had much foreknowledge, but could prove nothing. I didn't want to mention the name of Hampton. I had to say something believable.

'Who did Mr Combe call?'

'Do you think that's important?'

I responded with an empty phrase; however, I didn't know what the correct reply was.

Jones had a higher rank, and I could not order her. When she decided to send an announcement, I nodded. What did I do? I remembered well Gibbens' words, and I hoped he didn't intend them as a threat. That police news was published in the local newspaper, announced on the radio and local TV channels. Jones hoped we had a chance, the somebody-had-to-see-something hypothesis. I was more sceptical than she.

We read the reports over and over again. It was about 7 pm when Jones suggested continuing next morning, and I agreed.

'I think tomorrow we'll have some witnesses. Good night, Chief Inspector!' she waved. Rahul Bhatt already waited for her in the corridor.

They hurried away. I just walk very slowly.

When I stepped next to Mini Cooper, my phone started to ring. That was Shirley. I thought I forgot a dinner invitation—it really was possible.

'Sean... Jimmy... My God! Jimmy was hit by a car. We are in Norwich University Hospital now. He's unconscious and has two broken ribs.'

'I'm leaving right away...' I answered with a few empty phrases. I had to know what happened, but I was sure that was not an accident.

The young Stevenson was lying in the hospital bed, and he was white as the bedclothes. There was an IV tube and other similar things; I knew not which was what. Sirley and Doug stood next to him. We had a short conversation about Stevenson's physical condition, and I managed to learn with a few cross-question the correct circumstances of that accident. A dark car without a registration number drove straight at him—the witnesses said that. According to the doctors, he woke up soon, but he also suffered a mild concussion—at least that was encouraging.

I was shaken. I felt that was my fault—my hands were soaked in blood again. Obviously, they wanted to send a message what I understood well. I was confused. I needed fresh air and a little time to think.

'Do you want a coffee or tea?'

'You're kind, Sean… I must stay here… he wakes up at every moment…' explained Shirley in despair. 'Two coffees, please, with milk, no sugar. Thank you, Sean.'

'Not at all' I nodded.

I took a short walk, a tour around the hospital building. There was a garden for the patients in the backyard with trees, bushes and benches. I heard a fountain a little further. Some street lamps lit the garden; that's why I preferred to stay in the shadow of the building. I leaned against the wall and already regretted that I quit smoking years ago.

∎—∎—∎—∎▢∎—∎—∎—∎

We stayed with Stevenson all night. About 2 am, he woke up. We talked with him for a few minutes, and then he fell asleep. After that, I sent Sirley and Doug home, and I watched the young Constable. We agreed they were the day shift. I sat on a terrible hospital chair, and I thought that was my penalty because I had remorse. Sometimes later, I napped and my phone's ring woke me up.

That was Jones, and she suggested in that situation—regarding Stevenson's accident—I operated in Lower Oak, didn't deal with Abby Combe's case. I thanked and agreed with her. I think she truly worried about my young constable and offered her help if I needed. My daily routine started then. A few minutes later, I had another call from Norwich. A Superintendent—I didn't recognise his name—asked me why I dawdled in the hospital, why I was not in Lower Oak in my district. He didn't think that my reason could be appropriate and ordered me to Lower Oak immediately. So I didn't want to leave alone Stevenson, and there was one more call. That time I called Father Wilson, who asked no questions and was there in one hour. How did he do? I cannot imagine.

Shortly afterwards, the Mini Cooper turned onto the road towards Lower Oak. I received an SMS. It was very quick and essential: *We said no press.*

Yes. Thank you. I already understood.

EIGHT

IN THE MORNING, it started raining again. I had a bad mood, and that weather *enhanced* it.

I sat at my desk and tried to work on something when the electricity went out. Sergeant Taylor said it was usual on rainy days. Perfect. We were a dark place… It's true we could make tea because we had a gas cooker—our sense of comfort remained. The new circumstance did not prevent Taylor's activity, but mine very much.

Because my office had a large window, there was some light. I had a cup of tea and a deck of French-suited playing cards. I began a special solitaire card game: *Who is the murderer?*

Doctor Stemming was the King of Spades—spades and scalpels are similar, also pointed objects. I thought he was not a murderer, but an accomplice, yes. I was sure he had cut the body so that they could move it simply. Shirley told me before he had an expensive five and daughters—he might do anything for the money that the Hapmtons asked him.

The King of the Clubs—that was Reverend Hampton, doubtless. He had many good connections—for example, with the Anglican Bishop and some members of Parliament. He lived a very honourable life with an ordinary, boring wife and two sons—a dentist and a bookkeeper. Very honourable indeed, what could easily have been destroyed by a murder—he was the second on my list.

Doctor Jacob Hampton, the younger brother, a play-boy—he could be the King of the Hearts, of course. He was a lucky boy: no wife, but the girls and women loved him. He was handsome, successful and rich and had speeding offences, driving using a mobile phone; however, he didn't lose your license yet. By the way, he was third on my list.

Last but not least, the Mayor of Lower Oak, Mr Oscar Hampton, is the King of Diamonds. He and his wife—the Queen—had many shops in the town—for example, the *Hampton Tea House*. As Shirley mentioned, Mrs Oscar Hampton was a ruthless businesswoman—it's enough to think of the opening hours of the *Caffé Napoli*. Both of them—I mean Mr and Mrs Hampton—were Machiavellian and had first prize. They could lose a lot, and I thought they could do something to win. At the same time, there was the younger Oscar Hampton, the Jack of the Diamonds. He studied sociology or political science in Oxford—Shirley heard something similar. So we could determine in which year Abby Combe had been murdered, but in which season or month we could not. If there had been any romance between the young Oscar Hampton and Abby Combe that was an excellent motivation for Mr and Mrs Hampton to kill that girl, who may have been pregnant. The Jack of Diamonds was on my list also.

'Interesting card name. What is it?' Father Wilson stood next to my desk.

I didn't recognise him. I paid attention to my thoughts. 'Kings of Town' answered I hesitantly.

'I don't know this, but… beg your pardon' he said, pushed me a little further away and put the Ten of the Diamonds on the Jack. 'I'm afraid you didn't notice that card' he smiled at me.

'Thank you.' I let him finish it if it were a normal game.

After we drank tea with rum, I found some biscuits, so we ate them. I did not have an appetite, so that was enough for my lunch.

Wilson brought news. The young Stevenson woke up again, and they chatted a little bit. Stevenson remembered nothing. The doctors said that was usual in case of a head injury. The body was in shock, and that was the reaction of the brain. It was not certain that he could recall the information. I think Wilson thought I looked dejected about only the young Constable, and I did not want to oppose. So I asked him to visit Stevenson in the evening.

'My Superintendent ordered me to stay in Lower Oak, you know' explained I.

'No problem, Mr M… between us, that was a very stupid order… if not, you did something wrong.' He looked at me, smiling.

I gave no reply.

'Don't worry, I'll visit Jim Stevenson' nodded he. 'And I'll pray for you, Chief Inspector.'

Thanks, Father.

My office door was open, and I heard that something had happened. I thought to install a bell over the door to signal if somebody came into the station, as in a shop. Honestly, Sergeant Taylor was not suitable for that function. But who the hell would come here of their own free will?

About 3 pm, somebody came, but not from hell, just from the rain. He wore Wellington boots, British military raincoats from the Second World War and a storm fishing hat decorated with an embroidered Viking warrior—long beard, axe and helmet with horns.

'Somebody's here?' cried he, but Taylor snorted and did not awake.

I hurried out of my office.

'Yes, Mr...'

'George Pools, Sir. My name is George Pools, the younger. My father was the older, you know, but he died ten years ago. I stayed the younger George Pools yet.'

'Nice to meet you, Mr Pools.' We shook hands. 'I'm Chief Inspector Morgan. What can I do for you?'

Pools was surprised.

'It's very kind of you, Sir. I'm in big trouble, you know. Emily is missing, my little girl.'

I had many ideas in one second. It even occurred to me that there might be a connection between Abby Combe and Emily Pools.

'So, please tell me every detail, Mr Pools' I led him into my office. 'Take a seat, please.' I took out my notebook and a pen. 'I listen to you.'

Mr Pools sat in the chair, a little restless like a student taking an exam.

'Look, this morning I went into the stable, as usual. Charlotte and Anne ruminated peacefully, but Emily wasn't there.'

'Wait a minute! You said about Emily that she's your little girl. What did she do in the stable?'

'Yes, Emily, my little girl, Sir, as Charlotte and Anne. I bought them three years ago from a farmer. We keep animals, you know. We had these three cows, pigs and chickens. Many years ago, I had goats too, but they gobbled everything, even the barn's door. One of them was on the roof. I shot it. I hate goats. Ungrateful. But my little girls! My wife gave these names: Charlotte, Anne and Emily. I think from a romance novel or something else. Oh, my little girls! They give milk nicely, you know. They are so gentle, just that one, Emily wants to roam...'

Mr Pools spoke so much. First, I was angry. How did I prepare myself because of a cow? After I thought that distracted me.

'It would be better that we search Emily' I suggested.

I sought that little girl for four hours. Mr Pools lent me one of his bicycles and his German military raincoat. As I knew, that special equipment was part of his heritage. His father had fought in Dunkirk. The older Pools had been one of them who had gotten out. Pools' father had kept things as a memory and had collected other ones in Berlin in 1945. I suspected he had hidden a Luger or an SS bayonet somewhere in his attic. In addition, I learned a lot about the hen house's building, different forms of cow's milk processing and how I could make a perfect sausage. I think Mr Brown could meet Mr Pools.

When we returned to Pools' farm after our unsuccessful research trip, Mrs Pools welcomed us cheerfully. Emily came home three hours ago. Mr Pools was so happy and gave me a dozen eggs, a round cheese and a bottle of homemade gin. I didn't mean to hurt him, and then I accepted the gift.

It was still raining. The sky was grey, and it started to get dark. Luckily, the way back was relatively straight; otherwise, I could have easily gotten lost. I was about a few miles from Lower Oaks when I noticed another car on the road behind me. A big black car, perhaps a Land Rover Defender. It was approaching faster and faster, caught up and suddenly pushed my car off the road. Then the Land Rover stopped across in the middle of the road. I braked and turned off the engine.

The guy sitting next to the driver got out and came straight towards me. So it was the end game, I thought. Too bad I won't have time to drink Mrs Pools' delicious gin. The guy knocked at the car window. It doesn't matter whether I roll down it or not, because it isn't bulletproof.

'Somebody wants to speak with you, Chief Inspector' said he politely.

All right.

I got into the Land Rover.

On the back seat, there was an old-fashioned gentleman-looking guy in a long black overcoat with a Cartier watch and signet ring. Perhaps Mr Oscar Hampton himself? No. If he wanted to scare me, why could he meet me?

'May I introduce myself, Chief Inspector Morgan?' started the unknown man in a gentle voice. 'I'm the ex-Mayor of Lower Oak' he said, took off his black leather gloves and extended his hand. 'I'm afraid we have the same problem…'